UNITED KINGDOM OF RUSSIA

ALSO BY BRENT TOWNS

Team Reaper Thrillers

Fear the Reaper Series

The MI6 Files

Talon Series

Mark Hayes Series

Dave Nash Thrillers

Treasure Series

The Gods of War Series

Genocide

Congo Ice

Stalin's Spear

The Cuban Gambit

UNITED KINGDOM OF RUSSIA

THE GODS OF WAR
BOOK 5

BRENT TOWNS

ROUGH
EDGES
PRESS

Rough Edges Press
An Imprint of Wolfpack Publishing
1707 E. Diana Street
Tampa, FL 33610

roughedgespress.com

Paperback ISBN 978-1-68549-365-3
eBook ISBN 978-1-68549-364-6
LCCN: 2024946032

UNITED KINGDOM OF RUSSIA

MI6 INTERROGATION SITE, LONDON

FOR THE FIFTH CONSECUTIVE DAY, WE FOUND OURSELVES *waiting to face our grim-faced interrogators. The room we were in was slightly cheerier than the one we had started out in and had been in until yesterday.*

Today's agenda was to uncover the incidents faced by Knocker on his mission while I had been otherwise occupied in Cuba. As you should know by now, my name is John Reaper *Kane, my moniker originating from the Grim Reaper tattoo on my back. Beside me, looking fresh and cheerful, was Holly Smith, and I knew that once the questioning started, she would lose her joy and become just as jaded as me. Oh, and Raymond* Knocker *Jensen, who was in the hot seat beside her.*

The pair of them were Brits, but that's where the similarities ended. Knocker looked a little like me. We were the same height and build, roughly the same age, unshaven—his beard, like his hair, was a little lighter than mine—and we were both former military men. Holly, on the other hand, was a shade under six feet, had short blonde hair and a button nose. She was MI6 and had been our handler since the inception of our fight against the Russian generals known as The Gods of War. Fortunately, now there were a few less of them, having gone to meet their Gods.

We were seated at a rectangular conference table, and Knocker tapped impatiently while waiting for the others to join us. The atmosphere was charged with anticipation, all of us knowing that hostility would soon join with the arrival of the panel.

A quick update about our situation. The hearings were a farce. In fact, the whole intention was to flush out a mole called Hecate. This was the ultimate question mark hanging over the whole mission that had initially been set in motion in Syria.

Friends and colleagues had been lost in that time, but we had managed to thwart some grand but clandestine schemes along the way. Our unrevealed advantage was that we were in possession of Sergey Lash, the former president of the new USSR. After some interrogation, he had been convinced that talking to us was in his best interest. But it came at a price. There always was one.

We would produce him when the time was right. Until then, we would see our charade all the way through to the end.

"I'm sick of fucking waiting, Reaper," Knocker said to me, his voice low as the tapping on the table increased in intensity.

"They'll be here soon." I reached across Holly and stopped his hands from their incessant beat.

And they were. True to form, grim-faced, black-suited, the three politicians filed into the room. Charles German led the group, followed closely by Jack Holland and Christine Ryan. All were in their forties. Christine Ryan had been MI6 before the natural progression into politics.

The fourth member was CIA Director Ken Newman. Initially, he'd wanted me dead because of my role in something that had happened in Cuba. That animosity had accompanied him to London. Although I'd requested that he come, every time I looked at him in the first couple of days after his arrival, it made me want to bust him in the mouth. But since then, tensions had abated somewhat.

As the four adjusted jackets and sat down, Christine Ryan opened with, "Good morning. Director Newman has decided to stay with us until these proceedings close."

"Hey, Reaper," Knocker said with a smirk. "You know what the CIA stands for?"

"What?"

"Cunts, idiots, and assholes."

Newman gave him a withering look but maintained his silence. It was all part of the artifice we had in place.

I said, "Knock it off."

Knocker grunted. "Fine."

"Shall we get started?" German asked. "Since we're here to listen to Mr. Jensen's testimony, I think we may need an interpreter in the room."

Knocker pulled a face. "Funny prick, aren't you? How would you like to be added to the list of people who won't wake up tomorrow?"

German's expression changed. "I beg your pardon?"

"See, I can be fucking funny too."

Holly touched his arm. "Easy, Raymond. Let's get through today without any bloodletting."

"Fine," Knocker growled.

"Where are we starting?" Christine Ryan asked, her right eyebrow raised questioningly.

"That's easy," Knocker replied. "It starts with three dead men."

THREE DEAD MEN

Moscow was a dangerous place. Especially now that Sergey Lash was in control and had returned his country to the tyrannical days of the Iron Curtain. The streets were heavily populated by KGB agents, along with Lash's new Secret Police.

Craig Morrow, loath to leave the warmth of his safehouse, found it difficult to eschew the proposition of fresh intelligence. Especially when it was in reference to the upcoming British elections.

Snow fell lightly across the darkened Moscow streets, leaving a white blanket covering the ground. As he negotiated the icy sidewalk, Morrow's footprints marked his trail to the meeting place beneath the Novoarbatsky Bridge.

With just two weeks left to fulfill his current posting, Morrow was looking forward to heading home to his wife Ruby and seeing their two daughters in London. When he'd called earlier, he'd spoken at length with his wife about his imminent return if Whitehall didn't extend him again. He'd not had a chance to speak with his daughters as they had been out.

Passing beneath an orange streetlamp, Morrow appeared nonchalant, hands in pockets, gazing up at the flakes fluttering through the light beams like insects attracted to the brightness. He continued walking, stopping every so often to make sure that he wasn't being followed.

Something wasn't right. Morrow could feel it in his gut, and his skin prickled with anticipation. Stopping once more, he pulled back into the shadows of a storefront. He waited, his hand clasped to the butt of a Heckler and Koch P30SK handgun.

Morrow breathed deeply, trying to lower his heart rate and remain calm. He could hear approaching footsteps. Two sets, two people. Morrow's breath caught in his throat as he drew the handgun out and held it against his side out of sight.

Come on, you pricks, show yourselves, he thought to himself.

The footsteps grew louder, almost upon him. Morrow tensed, and then they were there. A man and woman, arm in arm, now laughing. The MI6 man looked down at his trembling gun hand. The pair walked on, oblivious to how close they had actually come to dying on this snowy evening.

Morrow waited until they had moved farther down the street before he stepped back out onto the sidewalk and kept going. Perhaps it was time to get out. Twenty years of this shit was starting to tell. He'd been to Syria, Egypt, Iraq, Iran, Myanmar, Mali, and Afghanistan. And those were just the good ones.

He and Ruby had often discussed life beyond MI6, the benefits of getting out. Maybe now was the time.

Up ahead, the wide expanse of the river lay black and oily against the white backdrop of the city streets. Heading to his right, Morrow turned toward the bridge. That was the predetermined point to rendezvous with his contact.

With the streetlamps illuminating the snow-covered landscape, Morrow could see no one else lurking around the stone bridge bathed in light.

Approaching the structure warily, he hesitated as a figure materialized from the shadows. It had to be his contact. As he drew nearer, he perceived that the figure was similarly attired to him, wearing a long coat and a hat.

Morrow stopped suddenly. There was something erroneous about the man's bearing. The MI6 man looked around, scrutinizing every shadow beyond the lights. His eyes failed to detect anything amiss, but every jangling nerve was screaming at Morrow to turn around and flee.

Sensing Morrow's trepidation, his contact began to walk toward him. In two minds prior to that, Morrow made the decision then to leave. He pivoted and hastily began retracing his steps, the P30 now in his hand.

"Mr. Morrow, wait," the heavily accented voice hailed him.

Morrow ignored it, putting his head down and deliberately lengthening his stride.

"Please, Mr. Morrow. I have the information you need."

Morrow hesitated, then stopped. He was this close.

Surely, he couldn't leave now. Turning back, he closed the distance between himself and the man who was his contact.

"Make it quick," Morrow said, looking around. "Something isn't right."

"Yes," the contact said. "I agree."

The black handgun in the man's gloved fist fired twice, the dull sound not the only thing bringing Morrow to a sudden stop. The air whooshed from his lungs, and he felt as though he'd been punched by the reigning heavyweight champion.

The MI6 man glanced down, horrified at the sight of a dark stain forming around two holes in his coat. Looking back up in disbelief, Morrow stared askance at his contact. The figure stepped forward, vanquishing the shadows covering his face.

Morrow's brow furrowed as he died, contemplating where he'd seen the man before.

Teddy Allen was the next person to die. The analyst for MI5 was investigating financial terrorism. An expert in his field, Teddy was forensically examining transactions linked to several different shell companies owned by various Russian corporations. Prior to his death, he'd discovered that hundreds of millions of British Pounds were being funneled into numerous shell companies owned by fake British corporations.

From there the funds accumulated in the accounts of just one. A company called United Holdings. Teddy had been looking into the stockholders of the company, but so far, he'd been unable to crack it.

Whoever was behind it all had done well covering their tracks.

Leaving work that evening, Teddy had stopped off at a restaurant for a bite to eat on his way home. He'd ordered the Chicken Tikka Masala and washed it down with two glasses of white wine.

When his lonely repast was complete, he signed the check and left the restaurant, hailing a cab on the street. It wasn't until he felt an overwhelming fatigue come upon him that he realized there was something wrong. By then, it was too late. Slumping sideways, he blacked out on the back seat of the cab.

An hour later, when Teddy awoke, he found himself tied to a chair, his retinas burning from a set of small floodlights. His captors had set up their interrogation in an old warehouse.

Their initial line of questioning regarded what he'd uncovered during his inquiries. When he didn't respond, they intensified their interrogation to torture.

By the time they had finished, Teddy had told them all he knew. Days later, each of the shell corporations had been closed down and new ones opened.

Once Teddy was of no further use to them, he was killed with a bullet to the head, and his body was dumped in a dark alley in London's west.

The body was discovered the following day by a police officer who called it in, and a detective was allocated to the case. Because the detective was close to retirement and intrinsically lazy, no real effort was made to identify the body. As there was no wallet or ID on Teddy, it was classified as a brutal robbery gone wrong. The killers had intended it to appear that way. Teddy was now in the system as a John Doe.

MI5 didn't find their man until a week later. He was still in the morgue with a tag on his toe, and no one any the wiser who he was.

———

MP Winston Jones was the final victim of the three. His demise by any means was deemed necessary due to the fact that he made too much noise and was outspoken against Fergus Pridham, digging into Pridham's family. When advice regarding his investigations reached those involved, a contract to silence the British MP was issued.

Jones symbolized a clear and present danger to the plan. The risk of what he might expose was not permissible. It was organized for an IED to be planted on the road that he frequently used in the commute to his office. When his driver reached the appropriate position that morning, the explosive was detonated with deadly efficiency.

Five minutes after the bomb had gone off, phone calls were made to several tabloids by a person claiming to be from a new branch of the IRA, claiming responsibility for the blast.

The good old IRA, a perfect scapegoat for any explosion in London.

The MP's death, along with that of his driver, was investigated by police and MI5, coming to the conclusion presented to them by the Russians, gift-wrapped with a bow on top. Liam O'Brien was a laborer from Belfast. But by the time the Russians had finished with him, he was an arms smuggler and a good friend of a bomb maker whose signature was found at the scene.

With O'Brien arrested as the main perpetrator, they rounded up an additional five so-called co-conspirators. All were locked away in a secure facility to be questioned by MI5. And while MI5 were kept busy interrogating the decoys, the Russians had their plans back on track, with all threats neutralized.

Nothing could stop them now.

Or could it?

CHAPTER 1

THE ONLY PASSENGER ON A PRIVATE JET TO WARSAW, Poland, I was on my way to a clandestine meeting with a former FSB officer. They had reached out to MI6 through archaic back channels. This was what I was born to do. Black ops were my thing. I'd been in the shadows more of my working life than I cared to count, and just the thought of a new mission had my excitement stimulated and feeling like an old friend.

Through the window, I peered down at the metropolis below. It wasn't my first visit to the city, and it didn't appear to have changed any that I could tell from this altitude. My last sojourn to Warsaw had been to kill a man. Ironically, he had been an FSB officer responsible for an assassination squad killing MI6 agents in the city.

Taking the better part of a week, I eventually vanquished the squad. My ultimate target being their commander, a man named, of all things, Vladimir.

This time, however, I was assured that things

would be different. Instead, I was to meet with the contact and then fly out straight away.

Supposed to.

When the plane landed, I was met on the tarmac by an MI6 officer.

"Hello, Mr. Jensen," she greeted me, shaking my hand. "I'm Mariette Sloane. Just call me Mary."

"Raymond Jensen. My friends call me Knocker."

She frowned instantly, stepping back before looking me in the eye and asking, "Why?"

I stared back, thought for a moment, and said, "Good question."

"You mean you don't know why?"

I guess her looks suited her demeanor. Short dark hair, attractive, but serious face, athletic, and wearing a pantsuit, not jeans and blouse. Very official. "Are you the lady in charge?" I asked, just making sure before I continued.

"No."

"Thank fuck for that."

"What do you mean?"

"You need to lighten up, Mary. You're as serious as a bloody funeral."

"The situation calls for it, sir," she replied.

"Don't call me sir."

"Mr. Jensen."

"Don't call me that, either."

"Raymond?"

"Definitely don't fucking call me that."

"Then what shall I call you?"

"Anything you like, except for those three."

"Ray?"

I nodded. "Ray I can take."

Climbing into a black BMW SUV, we were soon departing the airport vicinity. With only sporadic traffic on the road, it was far from as overcrowded as I was used to. Glancing over at Mary, I said, "I was told you'd have something for me."

"Glove compartment."

Pulling the latch, it opened smoothly, revealing a Glock 19 with spare ammo and magazines. I grinned, then withdrew them, concealing them on my person. Also provided was a suppressor, which I took and pocketed. "Thanks."

"What's the latest?" I asked Mary.

"Russian troops are proliferating along the border," she informed me.

"They're what?" The look I gave her intimated that she'd just sworn at me.

"Increased? It's not just a small contingent, it's fairly substantial."

Continuing through the streets, I looked out at snow on both sides, the plows having cleared them earlier in the day. The heaps were melting under the afternoon sun, leaving puddles in places.

Drawing closer to our destination, we crossed a set of tram tracks.

"Your room safe contains a folder. The combination is the last six numbers of your room receipt. Everything you need to know can be found in that file."

"What? You won't be dining with me tonight?"

"Is that all you think about?" Christine Ryan interjected, giving Knocker a scornful look.

"That didn't take long, did it?" he replied.

"I'm not surprised," she shot back at him.

"For your information, that wasn't what I meant. Now, can I continue?"

"Please do."

"Are you trying to get into my pants, Ray?" Mary asked me.

"Those things are that tight, Mary, I don't think I would fit."

"They aren't that bad," she replied.

"Then don't assume you know someone when you don't," I replied. "I just thought you might have dinner with me and catch me up."

"I-I'm sorry that I got you wrong," she apologized.

I shook my head. "No, you didn't. I'm just not that far advanced with you yet."

She laughed at my candid response, and I joined her.

Mary said, "Then I shall join you for dinner, Ray, and I'll *catch you up.*"

She let me out in front of the hotel, and I lugged my duffel inside, walking to the polished wooden reception counter. A young woman smiled and indicated that she was ready to serve me. "Welcome to our hotel. May I help you, sir?" she asked in heavily accented English.

"You have a reservation in the name of Grayson?"

"I will check." She looked down at her computer screen and looked up again, saying, "Yes, sir, I have it here."

After checking me in and passing me a keycard and my receipt, she asked whether I needed assistance with my luggage and wished me an enjoyable stay when I told her I had it under control.

Taking the elevator to the fourth floor, my sense of

smell was assaulted as the doors opened by the heavy floral fragrance of a carpet deodorizer. Possibly some kind of rose bouquet or fields of flowers. Whatever it was, it was sickly sweet and smelled cheap.

Following the hallway, I counted off the room numbers until I found mine, waiting until the door beeped as the lock disengaged with a swipe of the card. The same sweet smell hit me as the stale air from inside the room rushed out. Closing the door behind me, I looked around and then placed my duffel on the sofa.

The room was large, with a separate bedroom and a balcony overlooking the street. Not that I was willing to brave the chilling wind that hinted at the prospect of more snow.

Rummaging through my duffel, I picked out some clean clothes and headed for the shower, undressing while the water heated up. As I stepped under the spray, the hot water felt like fine needle pricks on my skin.

Using the dispenser shampoo, I washed my hair and then lathered my beard. It was getting longer and needed another tidy. I made a mental note to visit the barber when I got back.

Shutting off the water ten minutes later, I stepped onto the mat and dried off under the heat lamps. They felt like hot towels on my skin.

Once dressed, I went in search of the room safe. I tried the last six numbers on my receipt, as Mary had told me, and the safe opened with a beep. As promised, the folder was inside, so I removed it and took it over to the small table.

Opening the file and spotting the photo on top, I

knew this wasn't going to be as straightforward as I first thought. The man I was supposed to meet was dead. How did I know? Because I was the one who'd killed him.

———

In the restaurant, I threw the photo on the table in front of Mary and said, "Is this some kind of fucking joke?"

Her jaw dropped as she hurriedly turned it face down. "Are you crazy? What are you doing?"

The restaurant was half a block down the street from the hotel. Avoiding the one at my hotel because it looked too posh. I also didn't want to shit in my own backyard if there was trouble. Seems to me now, that was a good choice.

I took a seat. "This man is dead."

"Not if you're going to meet him, he's not," Mary shot back at me.

"Of course he is. I bloody well killed him."

She leaned in close and hissed, "Keep it down, blast you."

"Then tell me what is going on!" I snapped at her.

"All I know is that we received word through channels that this man wanted to talk to you, and only you."

"When?"

"Three days ago."

The waitress came over to our table. "Would you like to order?"

We looked up sheepishly because we hadn't even looked at the menus, then hurriedly placed an order and picked up our conversation when the waitress walked away.

Mary said, "When did you supposedly kill him?"

"Five years ago. I was sent to Berlin to kill Yury Gazinsky. He was an FSB assassin responsible for the deaths of an MI6 officer and two scientists who'd been helping defect to our side. They failed to make it to the pickup. Their bodies were found in a creek outside of Berlin."

"And Yury was the man responsible?" Mary asked.

"Yes."

"And you completed your mission?"

I nodded. "I managed to draw him out into the open and shot him in the face under the Brandenburg Gate."

"And you're sure he died?"

"You get shot in the head and see how you go," I growled in a low voice.

"Stranger things have happened," Mary pointed out.

"I guess I'll find out tomorrow," I said.

The arrival of our meals signaled the end of our serious discussion, and we made small talk while enjoying the food, imbibing a glass of red wine. I looked over the table and asked her, "How are you getting back?"

"Back where?" Mary asked, putting her almost empty wineglass on the table in front of her.

"Back to wherever you are going?"

"I have a small flat not far away. I'll walk."

"I'll escort you," I said.

Mary smiled at me. "I'll be fine, Ray, I'm a big girl."

"I'm sure you are, but in the time we've been

sitting here, I've clocked four suspicious people. One woman and three men. Two are dining as a couple, the others are sitting alone."

"You'd better make that six," Mary suggested. "There are two women eating together over your shoulder."

"I guess we're popular," I said with a smirk.

"What do you suggest?" Mary asked in a low voice.

"I'm curious as to why they sent so many."

I reached for my cell and made a call. "Hey, Knocker, what's up?"

"I need your help, Slick. I'm trying to rectify a disadvantage I seem to have found myself and a friend in the middle of."

Sam *Slick* Swift, what a guy with computers. You need anything hacked illegally—

"*Ahem?*"

"*What?*"

"*What do you think, Mr. Jensen?*" Christine Ryan asked.

"*Oh. I see what you're getting at.*"

Slick was a mighty dab hand with a computer. Solved problems whenever they arose. "Tell me your problem, Raymond."

"I'm in a restaurant and I need you to run facial rec to see if anyone is in the system."

"Does it have video?"

I hadn't thought of that. Glancing around the restaurant, I made out several cameras. "Yeah, three that I can see."

"Tell me where you are, and I'll see what I can do."

I gave him the details and then hung up. Mary looked at me and raised her eyebrows. "Friend?"

I nodded. "Old friend. Do you have a weapon?"

"I do."

"Don't take this the wrong way, but can you use it?"

"I have done a time or two."

"Good, you may need to again."

My cell rang as Slick got back to me. "Okay, I was able to get in, but the footage was pretty shit."

"What did you get?"

"All the ones I could identify are new KGB. Which means—"

"Someone told them I'm here, and I'm in the proverbial shit," I finished for him.

"Yes. What was it you always say? If in doubt—"

"Shoot someone."

"I was thinking of something else, Knocker."

"I wasn't. Thanks, Slick."

"Good luck."

"Yeah."

I disconnected the call and Mary stared at me over her tilted wineglass as she took the last sip and then placed it back on the table. "Well?" She raised an inquisitive eyebrow at me.

"New KGB," I told her. "This could get messy. I will, however, need one of them to question."

"Plan?"

I stood up. "Be right back."

"What are you going to do, Ray?" she asked.

"Bathroom."

The Glock was in the waistband of my jeans but was the last thing I wanted to use. As I walked away from the table, I speed-dialed Slick and said, "I need you to shut down the cameras for me right now."

"On it."

Two of the KGB people I had picked out rose from their tables and began to follow me, buttoning their jackets as they moved. I found the gents' bathroom and pushed through the squeaky swinging door. Thankfully I was the only one in there, which made what was to follow less complicated.

Hurriedly I screwed the suppressor onto my weapon, then waited out of sight in one of the stalls. I heard the door to the bathroom squeak open and then the footsteps crossing the tiled floor. Next were the voices, both Russian, whispers echoing in the hollowness. I set my jaw firm and made my move.

Stepping out of the cubicle, I shot the first man in the head, his brains spraying across the wall behind him. This was no time to mess around, that's how you get killed. His friend, I shot in the leg. After witnessing the unexpected and violent demise of his companion, he was shocked and slow to react.

Buckling to the floor, he commenced a painful squirming. Crouching beside him, I placed the suppressor under his chin. "Who are you?"

He glared at me through the pain.

"Who sent you? Was it Shatov?"

This time, I glimpsed a flicker of recognition in his eyes. Then I shot him in the head. I was certain he would not be further forthcoming, and I didn't have time to extract the information. I exited the bathroom and pulled the fire alarm on the wall.

The alarm started its clanging and whooping sound and people were getting to their feet and looking around in panic. I spotted Mary through the confusion and fell in beside her. "There you are," she said. "What happened?"

"The Russians are going to come up two short."

"Really? You killed them?"

"I got some information before I killed the last scouser."

"Such as?" she asked, looking around.

"They were sent by Shatov."

"Who?"

I was suddenly aware that Mary hadn't been read all the way in. I said, "I'll tell you later. Right now, we need to get out of here before Boris and Natasha take a run at us."

We slipped out onto the sidewalk and turned right, heading toward the hotel. Looking back, I noticed the man and woman following, not even attempting to hide the fact that they were trailing us. Turning the corner further back came the two women who'd been sitting behind me in the restaurant. I needed them to stop, to have enough doubt in their minds to make them think twice and break off the tail.

"I need you to kiss me," I said to Mary.

"What?"

"Just do it," I said to her, grabbing her hand and pulling her into my arms. Moments later, we were in what might be considered a passionate embrace, our lips locked together in a kiss reminiscent of an old 1950s movie. I was facing the way of the oncoming threat, able to keep an eye on them.

When they reached me, I made my move.

Separating myself from Mary, I stepped clear of her and brought up the suppressed Glock. I shot the man in the leg, sending him crumpling to the sidewalk. Before he was even on the cold, snow-covered pavement, I had changed my aim and pointed it at the woman. "Okay, think seriously about your next move. Your friends are dead. Your pal here is lucky. Turn around and walk the fuck away."

Her eyes blazed and her jaw set firm. Beside me, Mary said, "Two coming up behind."

"I'm a bit busy."

Turning her back to me, she brought up her fist, full of her own weapon and pointed it at the other two women and said in fluent Russian, "Stand where you are."

They stopped.

I said, "Pick up your friend and piss off. Tell Mikhail Shatov to send someone better next time. If I see you again, I'll not be so forgiving. I'll kill all of you. And as you have just learned, I have some experience with that."

They helped their friend to his feet and then backed away under the cover of both our weapons. Once they were gone, I turned to Mary. "I'm going to need another place to stay."

She nodded. "I can fix that."

CHAPTER 2

"Nice place," I said to Mary the following morning once I had showered and dressed in yesterday's clothes.

"You said that last night. Breakfast?"

"That would be great, thanks," I replied.

"What would you like?"

"What do you have?" I asked.

This would be where she'd tell me yogurt, cereal, juice, grains, and nuts. "You can have bangers and eggs, bacon, toast, coffee?"

Man, did I have her wrong. "Big day. Bangers sound good."

So, she heated a pan and cooked bangers and eggs for us both. They were pretty good too. "What do you plan to do today?" Mary asked me.

"Go to the meet and see what the hell is going on. I'd also like to retrieve my duffel from the hotel if possible."

Once breakfast was done, Mary quickly tidied up the kitchen before leading me downstairs and then over to the embassy. All of us. By that, I mean our Russian tail as well. Once through the security checks, Mary took me to meet her boss, Pete Evans.

A man in his late forties, Evans had been in Warsaw for the past five years.

"Who did you piss off?" I asked him when we met.

"I requested to remain here after my stint was up. I like being on the front line."

"You're possibly about to get a front-row seat to a bloody ground invasion," I pointed out.

"Very possible," he replied. "Mary says you have an issue with the meeting today."

"She told you about last night?" I asked.

"Yes. Very unfortunate."

"Unfortunate, my fucking ass. The bastards knew I was coming."

"Not from this end," he assured me.

"Fine, let's not worry about that at the moment," I said. "The man I'm supposed to meet today is dead. I killed him."

"When? Last night?" Evans asked.

"No, about five years ago under the Brandenburg Gate."

"If he's dead, then—"

"I don't know." It was a dumb question, and I was becoming increasingly sick of hearing them. "How about you tell me how you came by the intelligence?"

"It was brought to us through a contact with Polish Intelligence, in the form of a voice recording."

I frowned. "Why don't I fucking have it?"

"We didn't want it in the file."

"Why?"

"Security."

"Can I hear it?"

"Give me a moment."

Evans typed some commands on his computer, and moments later, a familiar voice was speaking to me.

"Hello, Raymond, my old friend. It has been a while since we last talked. But I guess that is all water under the Brandenburg Gate. See, I made a joke. I need to meet you, it is important. What I have is for you alone. It has to do with some high-ranking men you already know. The Generals..."

"Turn it off, I've heard enough."

I stared at the computer, my thoughts mixed and confused. "Jensen?" Evans said.

"It's him. I would know that voice anywhere."

"So, he's not dead," Mary said.

"They could have used AI to imitate his voice to send the message," I pointed out.

"They?" Evans asked.

"The Generals."

"Tell me about them."

"Could take a while," I replied.

"The condensed version?"

So, I gave him a redacted version of events. When I was finished, he asked, "Do you want some backup?"

"No, I'll have my own."

"Still, I'll send Mary with you. Just in case."

I wasn't happy about it and let him know. "Listen, these assclowns have killed a lot of people recently. They seem to be one step ahead of us all the time. I don't want anyone getting killed on my account. I'll be fine."

"Then at least let me give you some wheels."

"Fine."

I had a bad feeling.

―――――

Sometimes, when I get wound up about things, I like music to even things out. My choice for the drive to the meet was AC/DC. It didn't matter what song, just as long as it was loud. The BMW X5 seemed to rock with the beat.

The scheduled meeting place was the old town square. Parking a full block away, I ventured in on foot. Approaching my destination, I said, "Slick, old mate, what have we got?"

"I'm running facial rec. on everyone I see, and I've come up clean so far," he informed me. "But that doesn't mean they're not there, just that I haven't come across them yet."

"Roger that."

The square was laid with cobblestone-like pavers. At its center was a mermaid holding a shield and wielding a sword. An iconic symbol in itself. One depicted on Poland's coat of arms. I guess you learn something every day.

Crossing to one of the outdoor cafés, I sat down at a cloth-covered table. A waitress soon approached me and asked for my order. She had to do it twice because I wasn't too good on my Polish. I ordered just a coffee, white, three sugars.

"You got your ears on, good buddy?" Slick said over my comms.

"Do I need to shoot you, Slick?"

"Don't like it?"

"Fucking terrible."

"I thought it was rather good. Reaper would have liked it."

"Reaper would have shot you without warning."

"Fine. I have a table across the square with two men and a woman seated at it. Nikita Demenko, Igor Bokov, and Alina Fedorova. All are aligned with the new KGB."

"Keep an eye on them."

"Roger."

So, my wait continued. And things only got worse. "Knocker, copy?"

"Yeah."

"Looks like you've hit the jackpot. You're in the middle of a relative who's-who of KGB spies."

"What do we have, Slick?"

"Twenty no less."

I was impressed. Either I was in a trap, or Yury was still alive and at the top of Russia's most wanted list.

"It seems that someone is a very popular person," the voice said from the table behind me.

Well, I didn't see that coming. "Hello, Yury."

"Hello, Raymond."

"Been a while."

"Since the last time you shot me."

"Can't see how you survived it," I said.

"It was a long road."

"Why am I here, Yury? Is this a revenge plot?"

I heard him chuckle. "They are here for me, Raymond. Because I know things."

"What things?" I asked him.

"You'll have to get me out of here to find out."

"Slick, I need an exit," I said into my comms.

"Take your pick. They're all covered."

"Fuck." I made sure my weapon was ready and asked the Russian, "You carrying a weapon?"

"Yes."

"Good, you'll probably need it. Follow me."

I got to my feet and began walking in the direction that I'd come in. Behind me, Yury did the same.

Slick said, "Your friends are starting to move."

"Can you block their transmissions?"

"Not without blocking yours," he replied.

"Do it."

"But—"

"No time to fucking argue, Slick. Just keep an eye on things and only break in if necessary."

"Roger that. Cutting now."

My comms went dead, and so did the Russians'. Ahead of me, I saw two suspicious characters move into the open. There were no visible weapons, but that didn't mean they weren't armed. And their intentions were clear.

A quick scan of our surroundings revealed six more moving in. "Fuck it."

Withdrawing my suppressed Glock, I brought it up and opened fire. Four shots. Two for each man in front of me. Both dropped like stones to the paved square.

"Wait," German snapped, causing Knocker to stop. "You instigated a gunfight in a crowded area full of civilians?"

"I wouldn't say instigated," Knocker replied.

"What would you call it?"

"I'd call it doing what I had to do to keep myself and my contact alive."

"From what I read in the report, you barely managed to do even that."

"Doesn't matter how you do it, just that you do," Knocker replied.

"Just allow him to continue," Christine Ryan chided.

"Fine," German grunted. *"It can't be any worse than Mr. Kane."*

"Don't fucking bet on it."

I gave Yury a shove. "Move."

We broke into a trot, our paths clear. Bullets began whizzing through the air, many cracking as they passed close. We escaped the square and increased our speed along the street in the direction where I had left the SUV.

With a sudden grunt, Yury stumbled. I slowed and looked back, watching him begin to go down. "Fuck."

I did a quick one-eighty and returned to his side. "Come on, Yury, get up."

"I'm not going anywhere," he replied.

There was a lot of blood. I turned to look for our pursuers, noticing the closing proximity of the Russians. My Glock came up, and I opened fire. Two of the runners stumbled and fell. But the others kept coming.

"Damn it." I pulled at his coat. "Come on, Yury."

"Leave me, Raymond. I'm done."

"What information did you have?"

"Boris Pushkin."

"What?"

"Boris Pushkin. Find him. He can help."

"The Boris Pushkin?" German asked.

Knocker nodded. "Yes."

"Sorry, Mr. Jensen, continue."

As he spoke, I could see the blood on his teeth. Looking up, my attackers had regrouped and increased the intensity of their pursuit.

A burst of gunfire set me in motion once more, but

before I'd covered three strides, I noticed a white van stopped in front of me. As the sliding side door came open and revealed a shooter manning a fixed machine-gun, there was no doubt in my mind that they were not friendlies come to save me. "You have got to be fucking kidding."

I broke left just as the weapon opened fire. Bullets chased me into cover behind a blue BMW. The vehicle shook violently under the incessant rounds impacting the luxury vehicle. The windows exploded and the tires burst under the fusillade. I looked at my handgun and cursed it. What I'd give to have a H&K 416 right then.

I replaced the almost spent magazine with a fresh one, slapping it home and charging it, ready to fire. In front of me, I could see the wild rounds from the machine gun wreaking destruction on a clothing sell-er's building. The storefront window shattered, and the display mannequins became casualties of this violent war. I made a mental note to say a prayer for them later, but for now, I needed to concentrate on staying alive.

My comms came to life as a familiar voice said, "Incoming."

A dark green Audi appeared on the sidewalk and screeched to a halt. "Get in," Mary shouted at me.

I may come across a bit thick at times, but I didn't need to be told twice. I ran to the passenger door with my head low, trying to avoid getting it shot off. I scrambled into the Audi, a bullet whining as it rico-cheted off the pillar near the front door. "What are you doing here?"

"You're welcome," Mary shot back at me, flooring the gas pedal.

The tires squealed as it rocketed away from the battle zone. Then it hit the slick ice patches and became an almost uncontrollable beast.

But somehow, Mary regained control and made the next corner. Behind us, the van turned and followed. Mary said, "In the back."

Turning in the seat, I saw what she was referring to. A compact Heckler & Koch G36C. "Nice."

Reaching over the back, I grabbed it, making sure I put a round in the breech.

Mary said in a dry tone, "Just don't shoot any civilians."

"I don't plan on firing until—"

The back window imploded, covering the interior of the vehicle in a shower of shattered glass. "Yeah, now would be a good time to start."

Reclining my seat as far as it would go, I turned and crawled into the back of the speeding Audi. Meanwhile, our pursuers were maintaining a steady rate of fire at us. What made the situation more perilous was the slickness of the streets. One wrong move, and we would spin. But Mary handled it like a pro.

I came up and opened fire at the closest of the convoy of three vehicles now following us. As bullets punched through the front windscreen, I watched the Mercedes swerve.

The rear end slid out and caught the rear fender of a parked car. It flipped around, and the vehicle rolled.

The car landed on its roof and spun in circles on the icy street. The one following it swerved to the left and went around its rear end, sliding out briefly before correcting. I sighted the G36 and opened fire once more. At the same time, Mary took another corner, and my bullets flew wide. I didn't have time to worry about collateral damage.

Glancing over my shoulder, I noticed that we were now on a long, straight stretch of street. Mary put her foot down. Behind us, the two remaining pursuit vehicles took the corner one after the other and increased their speed. I saw a figure lean from the passenger window and open fire, the bullets from his weapon chasing us like a swarm of angry bees along the cobbled street.

Rounds peppered the trunk of the Audi. I felt one pass through the back window, narrowly missing my head, and hammered into the headrest of the seat beside me. Opening fire once more, I saw the bullets punch into the front of the BMW leading the chase behind us.

Mary took another turn and the rear of the Audi slid out before wildly fishtailing as she overcorrected. It slid to a halt, broadside to the vehicles pursuing us. "Fuck a duck," I growled.

I flung the door wide and opened fire, emptying the rest of the magazine at the oncoming BMW.

The vehicle's windscreen disintegrated, and it swerved out of control, still careening directly toward us. Behind the wheel, Mary slammed the Audi into reverse and trod on the gas. It shot backward, and the BMW narrowly missed the front of our vehicle and smashed into a parked car.

I grabbed another magazine and changed out the empty. From there, I charged the G36 and leaped out just as the Russians who were still able scrambled from their wrecked ride. I brought the H&K to bear on the first shooter, a big man with what looked to be an AK-12. My G36 came alive and spat twice, both rounds finding flesh.

I changed targets to a second shooter while walking toward him. Two more shots and he was down. As he fell, his trigger was squeezed, spraying bullets harmlessly into the atmosphere. Inside the crashed vehicle were the driver and passenger, who were either trapped or injured. Ensuring their permanent elimination from the fight, I pulled my Glock and put two rounds into each of them.

Jogging back to the Audi, I was about to get back in when the white van appeared. The roar of its motor echoed along the street. I climbed into the Audi and said, "Time to go, Mary."

"Knocker, are you there?"

"About time, Slick, where the hell have you been?" I asked as Mary started driving again.

"Are you okay?"

"I'm fine. I'm about to give you a name. Boris Pushkin. Dig into him."

"What happened to Yury?"

"He's fucked. Just find me what you can on Pushkin."

"On it."

"Who is Pushkin?" Mary asked, taking another greasy corner.

"A name that Yury gave me to probe into."

I looked out where the back window had once been and saw that the van was falling behind. "We're losing him. Where are we headed?"

"Out of the city."

"What about the embassy?"

"Pete told me not to come back there. It would be the first place they bottle up. We have a farm outside Warsaw that MI6 uses. That was a specialist team there."

"Fine, put your foot down and let's get the hell out of here. It's going to be cold without that window."

CHAPTER 3

WE PULLED UP OUTSIDE THE STONE-BUILT FARMHOUSE surrounded by mud and a thin layer of snow. Every tree had been cleared for at least two hundred meters, creating a perfect field of fire. I looked it over, sensing it was somehow familiar. "I'm getting Gangs of London vibes."

"That was where they got the idea," Mary said.

"If you remember, it didn't work out so well for them."

"We have contingencies."

"They did too."

Overall, the farm was a base for at least fifteen people at any one time. Ten of those were special operators, while the other five were MI6. With our arrival, that brought the total to seventeen.

The interior was a typical farmhouse. The basement, however, had been retrofitted with everything required, including a comms room and a well-stocked armory. On the walls in every room were red stop buttons.

"What are these for?" I asked.

"They drop the steel plates over the windows and doors, just like Gangs."

"You said there were modifications," I reminded her.

"There are," a voice said from behind us. I turned and saw a grinning face. "I recommended them."

SAS Captain Polly Tailor was a tall, broad-shouldered man I'd served alongside in Afghanistan.

I nodded. "Polly."

"Been a while, Knocker," he replied.

"I take it you two know each other," Mary said.

"Aye," I replied. "Polly and I did some time in the sandbox together."

"And Africa," Tailor supplied. "What are you doing here, Mucker?"

"Upset a few Russians."

"Normal shit then?"

"Something like that. What are the modifications we're talking about?"

Tailor nodded. "There is an escape tunnel out of the basement. It runs two hundred and fifty meters into the trees. Also, outside, there are a few shallow mines that we can detonate from inside."

"Anything else?"

"Yeah, this whole place is wired to blow if anyone breaches."

"I guess you've got it covered."

"Yeah, you want a beer?" Tailor asked.

I glanced at Mary just in case she had anything else for me. "Go for it."

"Sure, why not?"

Showing me into the spacious living room, Tailor said, "I'll be back in a minute."

Already relaxing there were three others. Two men, who appeared to be operators, and a woman who was an MI6 field operative. They all stared at me. I nodded. "Ray Jensen."

The woman said, "I'm Gail. These chaps are Trent and Frank."

Frank stared even harder at me after hearing my name. "You the same Jensen that saved the king a while back?"

"Yeah."

"Shit, that was some work you and your friends put in."

"It was a bit hairy. But that is a whole other story."

Tailor returned with the beer and handed it over. He asked, "Whose wife did you fuck this time around?"

"I wish that was the case," I replied. "This time around, we're up against it."

"Up against who?" Gail asked.

"A bunch of generals who believe that Russia belongs back in the Dark Ages," I told her. "Then throw in Lash. We've been fighting them for a good while now."

"The build-up along the border?" Gail asked, an inquisitive eyebrow raised.

"Part of a bigger plan."

"So you're pissing in Lash's pool," Tailor said.

"Just as hard as we can."

"Who is we?"

"Me and Kane."

"Kane?"

"They call him Reaper. Best damn operator I've worked with."

Tailor nodded slowly. "Seems to me I've heard of him. He around too?"

I shook my head. "He's running down something else."

"Big?"

"R-12s."

"Shit."

We drank beer and talked about old times. For the next two days, I awaited news from Slick about my next move. Then, when it finally came through, things kind of went sideways.

———

"Slick, what do you have for me?"

"Boris Pushkin is in hiding. I'm still trying to locate him."

"Why?" I asked.

"Someone tried to kill him. He's an oligarch who spoke out against Lash," Slick told me. "He was tipped to be the next president of Russia. However, once Lash got in, a kill squad rocked up to his estate outside Moscow and they tried to terminate him."

"But he got away?"

"He sure did," Slick agreed. "One thing about having money, it can buy you a good force of bodyguards. And it can help you disappear."

"So you have no idea where he is?"

"Not at the moment. But I'll kick over a few more rocks and then who knows?"

"Find him, Slick, he fits into this somehow."

"I'll find him, never fear. Now for the bad news."

"Do tell."

My cell pinged and I tapped on the small picture icon, opening the JPEG file. The photo I was looking at showed a dark-haired man dressed in a Russian military uniform. "Who is he?"

"Meet former Colonel Stanislav Rebrov. Was Russian army, now he commands a company of mercenaries who work for Grigori Igoshin."

"I've heard of Igoshin. I'm going to take a wild stab in the dark and say that Rebrov is in Warsaw."

"Give the man a prize," Slick replied with more than a hint of sarcasm. "His people were involved with the incident in the square."

"Great, that's all we need."

"These people are well equipped, Knocker. Don't underestimate them."

"I won't. How's the boss getting on?" I asked.

"She's busy trying to coordinate everything."

"Reaper?"

"Busy being Reaper."

"Fine, let me know when you have more."

"I'll send you an intel package on Rebrov. Should be there soon."

"Thanks, Slick."

———

The package proved interesting and enlightening reading. Rebrov was a decorated war hero. Syria, Mali. Having had enough of slaving to earn a pittance for the country, he decided to chase the money. Igoshin put him in charge of a battle company right off the bat.

Mary found me going through the file. "Who is that?"

"Stanislav Rebrov," I replied.

"I know of him. Runs a company for Grigori Igoshin."

"Yeah, well, he's in Warsaw."

"That does not bode well."

"No, it doesn't."

"What else did your man find out?" Mary asked.

I said, "He did some digging on that name. Boris Pushkin. The man is like a ghost. Apparently, he pissed off Lash and had to disappear. I'm thinking that Yury was sent by him."

"But you have no idea where he might be lying low to find out."

"Not a clue."

"I'll get the boffins here onto it, many hands make light work and all that."

"Thanks, Mary."

Twenty-four hours later, something shook loose. And not in a good way.

————

I was dragged roughly from my slumber just after midnight by Polly Tailor. "Get up, old son, we've got an issue."

I rolled off the cot and said, "What is it?"

"We've got numerous heat signatures all around the farm."

"An attack?"

"That would be my guess."

I hurried down to the basement, which was

already a hive of activity. Judging by all the heat signatures, they were out there in overwhelming numbers. "Why haven't they attacked yet?" I asked.

"Your guess is as good as mine."

One of Tailor's men gave me a weapon, ammo, and some body armor. He also hooked me up with some NVGs. I heard Tailor ask behind me, "What's the status of the farmhouse?"

"It's all locked down."

"All right, get to your posts. They aren't going to wait around forever." He paused and said, "Comms check."

One by one, everybody checked in. With everything up and running, within two minutes, we found out what our visitors were waiting for.

"I've got an air asset inbound," a voice said calmly in my ear. "It's not one of ours."

I had taken up a position at a shooting port on the ground floor. The rest of the defenders were spread throughout the building. Decked out in full combat kit and carrying an MP5, Mary came in beside me.

"You okay," I asked her.

"I'm fine. Brings back memories of Afghanistan."

"You served?"

"Yes, three years. Then MI6 tapped me."

I nodded. "Don't forget to duck."

Suddenly, the darkness outside was shattered as two illumination flares were fired into the night sky. They floated down, gradually fading until they burned out, then everything went dark once more.

Mary asked, "What was that about?"

"No idea, but I don't think it was for anything good."

Within moments, a low whop-whop could be heard in the distance, growing steadily louder, then a jet-propelled lance came out of the darkness and hit the top of the farmhouse with devastating effect.

Under the impact of the explosion, the building rocked. Diving to the floor, searching for any form of cover, Mary and I upturned a solid wooden desk. My comms lit up as voices called in from everywhere. Through it all, I could hear Tailor's calm voice giving orders. Outside the stone house, the attackers opened fire.

An RPG shot across the open ground and smashed into the front wall near the door, opening a ragged hole big enough to admit our assailants. The explosion began filling the room with dust and debris. Hearing a garbled cry of pain nearby, I came to my feet. I said to Mary, "Stay here."

Entering the next room, I found two SAS operators down. One had taken the full force of the blast, which had torn him to shreds, and was dead. The second operator had been hammered as well, and although he was banged up, he was still alive.

"This is Knocker. I've got two down, second room, ground floor."

"Roger that. Status?" Tailor asked.

"One KIA, the other is in need."

"Roger."

Smoke was beginning to permeate the house, and I knew that something upstairs was on fire. Had I gone to investigate, I would have seen why. Half of the upper floor was gone. Men were down and the place was burning.

I looked through the hole in the wall and saw a line

of advancing fighters. A fusillade of bullets peppered the front of the house and blew through the opening. I brought up the G36 and opened fire.

An approaching shooter stumbled momentarily but stayed erect. I fired again for the same result. "Shit." Now I knew why they looked odd.

"Heads up, Polly. They're in full suit body armor."

"Roger that. Someone flip those fucking mines."

Moments later, the night erupted as the mines detonated. Snow and debris shot skyward, mixed with the shattered bodies of our attackers. Where the assault line had once been, there was now just a blackened crater.

The firing died down and then stopped as the attackers fell back. We took stock of our casualties, which totaled three dead and five wounded.

I moved back into the basement and found Tailor giving one of his men orders. "...the wounded into the tunnel."

"On it, boss."

He looked at me. "We're on our way up shit creek, Knocker. Suggestions?"

"When life gives you lemons, make lemonade, old son."

"Really?"

"He who fights and runs away, lives to fight another day?"

"Christ almighty."

"How about run like fuck?"

"Now you're talking." He said into his comms, "Listen up. Get the wounded into the tunnel. We're leaving."

Then, a bad situation became worse.

———

Everything had gone black. I'm not sure how long for, but as I dragged myself from the floor, there was a loud ringing in my ears. I staggered to my feet, my breath sounding loud in my ears. My NVGs had been dislodged but my comms were still open.

"Someone talk to me," I managed to get out between coughs.

"Knocker, get to the tunnel. Every man for himself," Tailor said. "We're done. That last missile did us in."

"Where are you?"

"I'm trapped at the back of the house. A beam came down on me."

"Shit. I'm coming to you."

"No, get out!"

Grabbing my weapon, I lurched toward the other room where Mary was. "Mary, are you there?"

I heard her cough and then she said, "I'm here."

She staggered out of the gloom. I said, "Get downstairs to the tunnel. I'm going after Polly."

"Be careful."

"I'll be fine. Got too much to do."

Hurrying to the back of the house, I saw that the flames were growing, and the smoke was thick. Debris was everywhere and the night sky could be seen above me.

"Polly, where are you?"

"Over here," he called out to me hoarsely.

When I found him, sure enough, he was pinned beneath a beam, as he'd said. "What the fuck are you doing under that?"

"Shut the hell up and get me out of here."

Leaning down I got my shoulder in position and put my weight under the heavy beam and lifted. Barely budging, I changed my position to do it differently. This time, the beam moved slightly, then enough for him to slide out before I dropped it.

"Thanks."

"You all right?"

"I will be when we get the fuck out of here."

"Where is everyone else?" I asked.

"Gone, I hope," he replied. "We've taken some casualties—"

A figure loomed up and opened fire, bullets flying wide. I threw myself at my G36, which was where I'd left it on the floor while lifting the beam. But Polly's handgun was out and moved faster, blowing off a handful of shots. The shooter rocked back, not mortally wounded, but it gave me time to get my weapon.

I hammered off a full magazine, which the killer took in the body armor. He sat down under the assault. I lurched forward. "Okay, motherfucker," I growled.

I grabbed an exposed grenade from his webbing, pulled the pin on it, and ripped off his Kevlar facemask. Stunned at the sudden assault, he hardly even moved. I rammed the grenade into his mouth, breaking teeth and mashing lips. Then I threw myself backward and shouted, "Get down!"

Tailor hit the floor beside me as the grenade blew. The killer's head disappeared along with a good portion of his body. As the blast dissipated, I dragged Tailor to his feet. "Come on—ah fuck!"

Through the opening in the rear wall, I saw a figure lumbering forward, the movements notably robot-like. There was a minigun in his hands.

The lethal weapon whirred to life and started to tear everything apart, red tracers slicing through the night like long, unrelenting lances.

The interminable onslaught had everything around us disintegrating before our eyes. Never have I hugged the surface of something so tight in my life. To rise even a couple of inches was inviting death. I started clawing my way toward the hallway. Tailor was close behind me.

The minigun seemed to fire forever, its seemingly inexhaustible rounds causing a torrent of debris to cascade on top of us. Then it stopped. Thank Christ it stopped.

I scrambled to my feet. "Come on, Polly."

Without hesitation and not looking behind us, we sprinted through what was left of the house until the stairs down to the basement came into view. The further we descended, the more apparent it became that we were entering a clandestine chamber of chaos. The last few MI6 people were hastily trying to destroy everything they could lay their hands upon.

Polly shook his head. "Everyone, get out. We've got contingencies."

One of the agents looked at him. "We need to destroy it."

"It will be. Now fuck off!"

Among such pandemonium, the decampment was surprisingly orderly. Tailor turned to one of his remaining men. "Pete, you got that satchel charge prepped?"

"Good to go, Kettle."

I laughed. Despite our plight being dire, I still laughed.

Turning to face me, Tailor's visage spoke volumes, then he growled, "Shut the fuck up and get out!"

"Polly put the fucking kettle on. I get it."

"Just shut up and go. Once we're in the tunnel, Pete, let her rip."

Entering the subterranean slip away, we increased our pace along the dimly lit thoroughfare. The musty smell was of dampness and dirt.

Each of us following the man ahead like a herd of sheep, we soon broke out into the open. It was at that moment that the charge in the house blew and brought what was left of it down.

I heard Tailor say, "Everyone keep moving. There's a chopper on the way."

Mary came up beside me and asked, "Are you okay, Ray?"

"Yeah, you?"

"I'm not sure. We lost a lot of good people."

"How many?"

"There are only seven of us left. Seven out of seventeen."

I nodded. "It happens. Come on, let's get out of here."

CHAPTER 4

THE HELICOPTER EXFILTRATED OUR SERIOUSLY DEPLETED team to Germany, where we were situated in Paderborn. Each person was thoroughly checked over, and the wounded were transferred to Ramstein, where US doctors would treat and tend their injuries.

The powers that be determined that, for her safety, Mary should return to London. After Slick reached out the next day and told me about Pushkin, she volunteered to go with me. I didn't say no.

"Maybe you should have," Jack Holland sneered at Knocker.

"It probably would have been best," I said, looking at my British friend.

"In Raymond's defense, you can't tell what might happen in the future," Holly said.

"Maybe he should have given it more thought?"

Once more, I felt my mood darken. Over the past two years, we'd lost more friends than anyone had a right to, and it affected us in many unseen ways. Without exception, *those were the sacrifices we were prepared to make that made us the black ops operators that we were.*

I sighed. "Once again, you show blissful ignorance—"

"Wait, Reaper," Knocker said. "The guy has a point. I should have thought before I took her along. Perhaps things might have been very different."

"You don't mean that. The one thing that people like us can never do is blame ourselves for what happens. We start doing that, then we're cooked. You know that."

"Yeah."

"Carry on, Mr. Jensen," Christine Ryan said.

Slick called me early in the morning. He'd been rocking the keyboard for hours on end, running down leads, finally getting a hit. I rolled over in bed, careful not to disturb the sleeping figure beside me. "Yeah, Slick?"

"I found him, Knocker. It proved difficult, but not impossible. I have him."

"Where?"

"Adamantas, Greece. The Island of Milos."

"Okay. Is Holly there with you?"

"I am," she replied. "What is it?"

"I'm going to need transport to Greece."

"You leave tomorrow. It was the earliest I could do it."

"You're a doll," I replied.

"No, I'm better than that. Do you need backup?"

I thought about it for a moment. If we had this much trouble finding Pushkin, the Generals weren't going to find him in a hurry. In and out. "No, I should be right."

"Fine, I'll have Slick send through the details."

"Thanks, boss."

"Stay safe, Raymond."

Disconnecting the call, I lay there staring at the ceiling.

"I want to come with you."

Rolling onto my side, I saw Mary staring at me. "Why?"

"You might need help."

"I'm better on my own."

"What if you get into trouble?" she asked.

"Better that I get into trouble on my own," I replied.

"Come on, Ray, all they're going to do is send me back to London. I belong in the field."

"What if I get you killed?"

"Then I've died doing something for my country," Mary said with determined finality.

I contemplated the matter seriously for a while before making a decision. "Fine, you can come. But you do what I say, when I say it."

"I'm a big girl, Ray. This isn't my first ruck."

"Let's hope it isn't your last."

———

Like many buildings on the islands of Greece, Adamantas hadn't been spared the special price on the purchase of white paint. Everywhere you looked. Every building. The stark white seemed to rear back and slap you in the face. I get that it's cool in the heat, but a man could get bloody snow blind in the damn place.

It felt good to be away from the real snow and the

bone-chilling cold. Adamantas was on the southern side of Milos.

Although we had the option to fly, we'd chose to come by boat. Upon disembarking, we found a car waiting to collect us. MI6 had set us up in a luxury villa for a few days, complete with an outdoor area and a pool. Not that we brought our swimming kit.

"Who needs that?" Mary pointed out when I happened to mention the issue. She started to peel out of her clothes.

"We have a job to do, remember?" I pointed out, admiring the view.

"Yes, but that is tomorrow."

I shrugged and began to follow suit. "True."

We jumped naked into the pool and slid across into each other's arms, our bodies—"

"I think we get the picture, Mr. Jensen," Christine Ryan said hurriedly.

Knocker shrugged. "I thought you wanted a broad picture."

"Yes, but not the intimate details."

I grinned.

He sighed. "Thank Christ for that. For a moment, I was thinking I'd have to tell you about the whipped cream thing."

"Please don't."

"No complaint from me. The places I ate that shit from—"

"Mr. Jensen, continue."

After the pool thing and other stuff, we dressed and headed out, located a nice café nearby, and sat down to enjoy a meal. I guess, looking back now, I should have picked up then that something was out of place. At a nearby table, a man and woman were too loved up. Even honeymooners don't carry on the way they do in movies.

I should have shot them then and there. But I didn't because I failed to make them.

With our repast complete, we sauntered back to the villa, enjoying the warmth of the late afternoon sun, the clearness of the azure sky, and the glimmering water in the bay. An hour after our return, there was a knock at the door. Approaching the door cautiously, I held my Glock hidden beside my thigh. Opening the door, I looked up to see a tall, broad-shouldered man standing in the opening.

"You are Jensen?" His voice had an Eastern European accent.

"Who the fuck are you?" I asked him, my grip tightening on the gun.

"Igor. I am here from Mr. Pushkin."

"Are we still meeting tomorrow?"

He shook his head. "No. Tonight."

"What's happening?" Mary asked, stepping into view with her handgun visible.

"There's been a change of plan," I told her. "The meeting is tonight."

"All right, let's go then."

"No," the man said. "Just you."

I looked at Mary. She nodded. "Okay."

Noticing the gun I was holding, he shook his head and said, "No weapon."

"Yeah, you can get fucked. I'm taking it."

After staring hard at me for a tense few seconds, he nodded. "Fine."

Turning to Mary, I said, "I'll be back soon."

We left the villa, taking a circuitous route for about thirty minutes, covering a distance that equated to two blocks. Normally a five-minute walk.

Surprise, surprise, we arrived at another white two-story home with greenery on the windowsills. Letting me pass through the door ahead of him, I walked deeper into the shadows of the cool room. In the living area, standing beside a heavy brocade sofa, wearing suits, were two men. I guessed that neither was the man I was looking for. This alone put me on heightened alert. If you go to meet someone, they should at least be there to greet you.

"Hey chaps, how's it hanging?"

They gave me a puzzled look. Then I said in Russian, "Where is your boss?"

"He is busy," the one on the right answered.

Right about then, I became acutely aware that positioned behind me was the man who'd escorted me over. Scanning the room, I noticed a bottle of vodka sitting on the counter of a wet bar, several glasses alongside it. "You mind if I grab a drink?"

The one in charge shrugged and gestured with his hand. "Sure, why not?"

His tone intimated that it would be the last before my execution. I picked up a glass, turning it over before pouring a generous portion of the clear liquid into it. Turning casually to face them, my back to the wall, I asked, "Is Yury around?"

Lifting the glass to my lips with my right hand, I studied them across the lip of the tumbler. Their gazes darted questioningly at each other, then finally back to me.

My grin was designed to unsettle them. It achieved that and more.

They went for their guns.

When the need arises, I can be quite ambidextrous, and I already had mine in my left hand. The Glock hammered and the leader died with two in his chest. The second followed seconds later the same way.

By this time, the third guy had reacted, his weapon out and in action, snapping off a couple shots. The first missed me and hit the wood frame of the mirror above the bar, lodging deeply in the wall behind. The second would have found flesh had I not already been moving.

Diving sideways to the tiled floor, I knew that the killer's shot had flown true, slicing the air where I had just been standing. My gunshot didn't miss, hitting him in the stomach and doubling him over. His weapon clattered onto the terracotta tiles.

Coming to my feet, I crossed the room to stand over him. On his knees, he was clutching his guts, his jaw clenched in pain.

"Who are you?" I asked him.

He groaned.

"Hey, cunt, who the fuck are you?"

Looking at me defiantly, he spat blood.

I shot him in the head.

After riffling through their pockets, I found nothing of any use. Reaching for my cell, I called Mary.

There was no answer.

My guts knotted.

I had a bad feeling.

———

Setting off at a brisk jog, I reached the villa within a few minutes. Silence greeted me when I opened the door, but I knew something was wrong. The Glock was in my hand before I stepped across the threshold. Moving silently along the short hallway, I soon came into the combined dining and living area.

My progress was halted when I spied Mary sitting with a briefcase on the dining room floor beside her. The lid was open, and I could see what was inside. "Looks like you're in a bit of a spot," I said to her.

"You could say that. I was hoping you'd be back soon or not at all."

I walked over to her. "Who did this?"

"The loved-up couple from the café. Do you remember them?"

"Yeah, how could I not. Almost made me throw up in my mouth."

She gave me a wan smile, appreciating my attempt to lighten the predicament she was in.

The countdown clock on the bomb ticked over the three-minute mark. I looked at the handcuffs. I had nothing to pick them with, and just looking at the bomb, I could see that it was fixed with anti-tampering.

"This is a little tricky," I said.

"I'm sorry, Ray. I thought I was alone, and then they were there."

"Don't worry about it. Let's just get you out."

Two minutes thirty left on the clock.

"Just go, leave me. There's no sense in us both getting killed. I'm expendable, you're not."

Staring into her eyes, I saw the fear and anguish there and made my choice. She wasn't going to die tonight, and neither was I. "Wait here."

I ran through to the kitchen, hastily searching each of the drawers. There was nothing I could use on the handcuffs. My heart was starting to race, knowing that we were running out of time. This wasn't happening.

I went back to the top drawer, looking down at three butcher knives. Grabbing the largest one, I raced back to the dining room, moving around behind Mary, keeping the knife out of sight.

"Did you find something, Ray?"

"Yes. I'll have you free in a minute."

"That's all the time—"

Then I hit her.

"You knocked her out and cut off her hand, just like that?" German asked, the horror in his voice evident.

"It was either that or leave her there to die," Knocker replied.

"But you hacked her hand off," he said angrily.

"And she is fucking still alive," he roared. *"There was no time. I did what I had to do—"*

"That is your answer to everything, isn't it?"

"Well, what the fuck would you have done?"

German stared at Knocker before he picked up the phone in front of him and said, "Send her in."

The door swung open, and Mary walked in. She was wearing a suit, and her left arm was in a sling, minus her hand. She stood at the end of the table, ignoring us and staring at the three inquisitors.

German said, "Miss Sloane, I trust you are on the road to recovery?"

"Yes, sir."

"Could you tell us what happened when you woke up in the hospital?"

"Well—"

"You want to put her through this all again, you bastard," Knocker snarled.

For a moment, I thought he was about to go across the table. "Knocker."

"Don't worry, Reaper, I'm not going to kill him."

Christine Ryan said, "How about we take a quick recess and then come back to it? While the others are gone for coffee, Miss Sloane can relate her version of events to us."

German nodded. "Yes, a good idea."

So, we went for coffee.

"Don't let him get to you," I said to Knocker. "He's an asshole, we all know it."

"I can't help it. I feel bad enough as it is."

"Have you seen her since we've been back?" I asked.

"No."

"She has asked about you," Holly said.

"She has?" Knocker was surprised.

"Yes. Maybe after this is over, you should go and see her."

"Maybe I will."

When our coffees were about finished, our attention was drawn to the doorway of the cafeteria as Mary walked in. She stood by the table and stared down at Knocker. I said to Holly, "We should go."

"No, it's okay," Mary said. "I just wanted to tell Ray that I don't blame him for what happened. He saved my life."

"Prick of a way to do it," Knocker said, shaking his head in guilt.

"If I had to go through it again, Ray, I'd hope you'd do the same thing. I told them that too."

"I'm sorry, Mary."

"Don't be."

Knocker hesitated. Then he said, "After we're done with all this, would you like to catch up for a beer?"

Mary nodded. "I think I would. Do you have a pen?"

"I—no."

"It's okay," Holly said. "I'll get him your personal number when he's ready."

"Thank you, Holly. Well, I must be gone. It's good to see you, Ray. Please don't blame yourself."

Knocker nodded. "Okay."

"Good. Bye, everyone."

We watched Mary leave, then finished our drinks and headed back up to the room. Settling back into our seats, we waited for proceedings to resume. I glanced at Newman. Throughout the whole first period of the day, he'd sat and maintained his silence.

German said, "Okay, let's continue. I believe Mr. Jensen was still in Greece."

There was nothing left of the villa after the bomb detonated. I delivered Mary safely to the local hospital, making sure she received the medical attention she needed, before calling Holly and giving her the rundown on what had transpired. That done, I headed back to the house where I'd left the dead people. Upon entry, I was surprised to find the bodies had disappeared. Everything else was there, the damage and stuff, but no bodies of those I'd killed.

I called Slick.

"Hey, Knocker, I heard what happened. Sorry you

had to go through that. Holly has dispatched a team to take care of Mary."

"That's something, I guess. I need your help."

"Name it."

"Someone took these bodies away. See if you can find a camera for me."

"Right away."

While he did that, I began poking around the house. Had Pushkin ever been here, he was long gone, which meant we were back at square one in the search to locate him.

"Knocker, I have something."

"What is it, Slick?"

"The two people in question left the villa not long before you arrived. You only just missed them. It looks like they had an escape plan because they went to the harbor and caught a boat off the island."

"Any idea where they went?" I asked.

"Athens."

"That has to be where Pushkin is," I said to him. "That's where I need to be."

"I'll look into it."

"Thanks. Let the boss know."

"Keep an eye on your six, Knocker."

"Yeah."

CHAPTER 5

THE FOLLOWING DAY, I WAS IN ATHENS. SLICK HAD figured out that Pushkin had been tipped off by someone the day before the scheduled meet, which was why he'd fled and headed to Athens. I was enjoying a takeout coffee while seated in the Monastiraki marketplace.

I studied the most current picture of Pushkin on my cell again. Slick had tracked him to somewhere in this vicinity. I was hoping that, with some luck, Pushkin would show up around the traps and I could follow him back to wherever he was staying.

In the background, Slick was doing sweeps of the area, running facial recognition on anything promising. So far all was clear, but I knew that could change in an instant.

"All clear so far, Knocker."

"Thanks, pal."

I took another slug of my coffee. It was strong and bitter and good. Up to the point where it was getting cold. That point was now. I guess I'd been sitting on it too long.

Getting to my feet I carried the cup across to a trash can and dropped it in, casually glanced around, looking back at the ruins I could see. Then I glimpsed the three men entering the square.

"Slick, three men entering the square to the east. I think that might be our man."

After a few moments, Slick said, "That's him."

"All right, let's see what happens."

The three men, seemingly relaxed, found a table at the outdoor café area and sat down. They ordered drinks, which arrived soon after. All the time, I watched and waited.

"They always seem to find a way, don't they?" Slick said with a sigh.

"Who does?"

"The bad guys."

"What have you got?"

"Four people, including the man and woman from Milos."

"Four doesn't seem enough," I said to him.

"My thoughts exactly. Give me a moment."

While I kept watch, Slick searched on his computer. And while we were both busy, the shit hit the fan.

I heard the sharp snap of a bullet passing above me. Then I saw the first of the two bodyguards buckle as a bullet hit him hard. "Sniper, fuck."

Lunging to my feet, I set out running across the square toward Pushkin and his remaining bodyguard. My Glock was in my hand, my legs pumping.

"Sniper! Sniper! Get the fuck out of it."

People started screaming, looking bewildered and

running in all directions. Ahead of me, a big guy turned to face me. He wasn't a bodyguard, and when he took out an MP7, I made the split-second choice to shoot him. The bullets from my Glock sat him on his ass. As I ran past, I placed the handgun to his head and pulled the trigger, finishing the job.

A running civilian crashed into me from the side and knocked me off balance. I gathered myself and pressed forward. Meanwhile, the sniper was still shooting. People were dropping left and right as he took out targets indiscriminately. There was nothing I could do about it.

Someone else hit me from the side, knocking the Glock free of my grasp. I hit the ground hard and rolled, coming up onto a knee. There, standing in front of me, was a woman. Lithe, athletic, skintight clothing that hugged the compact muscles on her frame.

She gave me a wicked grin, bringing her fists up. I spat on the ground and nodded, climbing to my feet. "All right, just remember, you called it."

I walked forward, and with the swiftness of a striking cobra, she spun and kicked me in the head. Once more, I was on my knees. This time, when I spat, it was mostly blood. She came at me again, swinging another kick. I lifted my arm to block the blow, but it didn't prevent me from being thrown sideways.

I let the force of the kick add to my momentum and rolled away. Regaining my feet just in time, I prepared for another assault. "Fuck a duck."

Two additional blows got me, both times with her fists. She could fight, I'll give her that, but she'd made a mistake by pissing me off. When that happens, I have to win by any means possible.

This time, when she came at me, I wasn't going anywhere. Her blow was aimed at my face, but instead, I dropped my head, and she broke her hand on my hard skull. With a backward step, she withdrew her hand, crying out in pain. I stepped into the void created by her retreat, sending a left hook toward her head. She blocked the blow, leaving herself open. My right streaked forward and socked her in the torso. My fist impacted her rock-hard abs, and I heard her grunt as she took another step back.

Then, emitting a deafening howl of frustration, she launched herself at me. With a flail of arms and legs, I managed to hook her arm with my own and hip-tossed her to the hard pavement. Groaning, she glared balefully at me. "Stay there," I growled.

Somehow, the silly cow kicked out with her legs and landed on her feet. She turned and faced me, ready for the next attack. I shook my head. "Oh, fuck me."

She came at me again, kicking, throwing punches like some fucking Russian Bruce Lee. I dodged and weaved and got hit. She kicked at me again. This time, I stepped forward, taking the blow on my ribs, and pinned her leg in place with my left arm.

Her face was one of frustration, while mine was almost apologetic. My right arm swept over and came down hard. I heard the bone in her leg break and let her go. She let out a piercing scream of agony as she fell.

I walked over to grab my Glock and said, "Slick, where is the target?"

"Gone west."

"Literally?"

"Uh, huh. Just head in that direction."

So I did.

While getting shot at.

Bullets cut through the air with more frequency than before. More civilians got hit before I managed to escape the shooting gallery. "Slick, where is he?"

"Continue going along that street, Knocker. He's somewhere ahead of you."

"Christ," I said as I saw the chaos in front of me.

"Knocker, you've got more trouble headed your way. Three vehicles. SUVs, dark blue or black."

"Fuck." I glanced around, searching for anything that might help my situation. To my right, a guy was unloading something from the back of a refrigerated lorry. Thankfully, it wasn't an articulated vehicle.

I climbed up into the cab and started it, eliciting a shrill shout from the rear as the driver ran beside it toward the front. I gave him an apologetic wave and started off.

"You stole a lorry," Holland glowered. "Just like that."

"Not only just a lorry," I said to him. "I purloined a motorized conveyance—commonly referred to as a lorry*—by orchestrating a sequence of surreptitious maneuvers, thereby appropriating it for personal use."*

"What?"

"Yes, I stole the fucking thing."

The lorry pulled away from the sidewalk with a roar as my foot went down on the pedal. The metal monster started swallowing diesel in copious quantities as it picked up speed. The running civilians in front of me started to part like the Red Sea when Moses struck his staff ahead of the pursuing Egyptians.

It was a couple of moments later when I saw Pushkin being helped along by his remaining bodyguard. I rolled down the window. "Boris."

He looked over at me, this guy he'd never seen before, driving a lorry. I shouted again, "Boris. Get in before they kill you."

Knowing that his options were limited, he hesitated only momentarily before running toward the vehicle and opening the door. His bodyguard helped him up but was not so lucky himself, catching a bullet as he was climbing in and falling back to the pavement.

I floored the pedal once more and the lorry lurched forward.

"Who are you?" Pushkin asked in bewilderment, pulling the door closed without a backward glance at the loss of his man.

"You mean you don't know?" I asked him.

"Wait." There was a moment of vocal silence before he said, "You are the one that Yury went to see. Jensen."

"That's me."

"Where is Yury?"

"He's dead. He gave me your name just before he died. He said you could help with whatever was going on."

"What is going on?"

"The Generals they call The Gods of War."

"Then maybe I can help you."

Gunfire erupted beside us as an SUV appeared. Bullets peppered the lorry and I swerved involuntarily. I corrected the steering and then cursed as I swerved once again. This time at the SUV, clipping it and forcing it to crash into a parked vehicle.

"What do you have?" I asked him as I made another turn.

"The information you need is in a bank security box. Get me out of here and I will tell you where it is."

Bullets peppered the lorry once more. "Really? What if one of these bastards shoots you in the meantime?"

"Just hope they do not."

"Fuck me," I growled, shaking my head. "This is bullshit."

Glancing at the side mirror, I saw the two SUVs following close behind. Shooters were hanging out the windows, firing their weapons. I felt like I was in an '80s action film surrounded by chaos and carnage. Swinging the wheel of the lorry, I clipped a parked vehicle, flicking it out into the path of those following. It wasn't much, but it was enough to slow our pursuers down slightly.

We were rushing toward an intersection, and I was forced to stand hard on the brakes. The load shifted in the cargo space as the tires juddered, leaving black rubber streaks on the pavement. I turned hard to the left, cutting out into traffic. A vehicle swerved and crashed into a parked car while another managed to come to a halt before anything major happened to it.

I floored the pedal again, the open doors at the back of the lorry swinging wildly. I saw some boxes fall out and roll across the street. One burst open and packets of something spilled out.

One of the remaining SUVs tried to pull up beside the truck. I saw him coming, gave him just enough rope, and then hung him. The lorry moved over and swiped the SUV. The driver reacted instantly and crashed into a streetlamp, bringing it down. It seemed to fold and came to rest across the vehicle's roof.

That still left one more SUV.

I glanced over at Pushkin. "You all right, Boris?"

"I am fine."

"Why do they want to kill you?"

"Because I know too much, and I do not fit into their plans."

"You mean their plans to return the USSR to its former glory?"

"Yes, but there is more. Much more. If Lash is not stopped or terminated along with the Generals, the world will burn."

"They're already two less," I told him.

"That was you?"

"Me and a friend."

More shots, and I swung hard on the wheel. This time to the right and I made the turn. Looking in the side mirror once more, I saw the SUV, but now it wasn't alone. It had been joined by at least two police cars.

Suddenly, the shooters turned their attention to the police and were sending heavy fire in their direction. I saw one of the police cars turn sharply and then go into a spin before slamming into a van parked in a loading zone.

"Fuck this," I snarled. My foot slammed down onto the brake pedal and brought the lorry to a screeching halt.

Behind us, the last SUV smashed into the rear of

the lorry, blocking the street. I looked over at Pushkin and said, "Right, out. It's time to go."

Pushkin scrambled out the passenger side, and we hurried to the front of the lorry. I heard the screech of tires and saw a sedan parked behind the remaining police vehicle. Three armed people climbed out. The two police officers turned and were cut down before they could speak.

I turned to Pushkin. "Go. Go now."

We set off at a run along the street before cutting onto the sidewalk. The Russian oligarch wasn't your average fitness fanatic and was not able to sustain much pace. Mind you, the bullets coming our way seemed to motivate him to more speed.

I turned and fired at one of the shooters who was standing near the front of the lorry. I saw him reel back and fall. The slide on the Glock locked back, indicating my need to reload. I dropped out the empty magazine and slapped home a fresh one.

One of the two remaining shooters opened fire, and I returned it on the run. I kept Pushkin moving along in front of me. "Slick, are you still with me?"

"Roger that."

"I need some guidance."

"Up ahead of you, you'll see a narrow laneway. Head down there."

"Left or right?" I asked.

"Sorry, left."

I picked it up. "Keep moving, Boris."

"Speak for yourself, Englishman. I am no longer a young man."

"And I'm too old to be getting shot at. Keep fucking moving."

We slipped into the laneway. I stopped while Pushkin kept going. He looked back over his shoulder. "What are you doing?"

"Just keep going, I'll catch up."

The Russian turned his attention forward and kept running. Meanwhile, I'd decided enough was enough. Peering around the mouth of the laneway, I saw the approach of the two shooters. I waited until they were almost on top of me then I stepped out.

The Glock crashed and the first of the two Russians went down. His momentum carried him into the wall of the building beside us with a sickening thud. Even as he fell, I was turning to the last one. I fired four times. Mostly through anger.

The bullets smashed into his chest, and he fell like an out-of-control ice skater. Hurriedly, I dug into my pocket and took two photos with my cell before turning and following Pushkin. "Slick, I just sent you two pictures. See what you can find out. Also, we're going to need extraction. I don't care how or where to. Just get Holly onto it."

"Already on it."

I caught up with Pushkin. "There's an extraction coming. But these guys aren't going to stop. I need to know where that lockbox is because if they get lucky, we're screwed."

Pushkin nodded. "The Bank of St. Petersburg."

"Ah, fuck me."

———

We sought shelter in an abandoned villa on the outskirts of Athens. It was tidy, but you could tell no one had been there for a long time. I looked at Pushkin and said, "Time to start talking, Boris."

The Russian oligarch nodded. "I have known Sergey Lash for years. Also, his relationship with the Generals."

"Yes, we know about his grandfather. What about Dolos?"

"Dolos is the codename for a Russian inserted into the upper echelons of the British government," Pushkin told me.

"Pridham?"

"Yes."

"How?"

"It is all in the papers I have."

My cell went off. "Slick?"

"Things have just escalated some here," he told me. "An IED has gone off, as well as a car bomb close to the heart of the city."

I was silent as my mind worked through the news. A car bomb was random, but the IED had a personal feel about it. "Tell me about the IED."

"Can't tell you much at the moment."

"Find out and dig into any other occurrences over the past few days. Something is off."

"Give me an hour or so, and I'll see what I can come up—" He stopped. "Shit."

"I knew he was working while talking to me because that was what he did. Talk to me, Slick."

"The IED targeted Winston Jones, MP."

"Who is he?"

"He was one of the most vocal opponents of Fergus Pridham."

I nodded. "There has to be other stuff, Slick.

Find it."

"What stuff, Knocker?"

"Stuff that only you can see."

"It has started, hasn't it," Pushkin said.

"Tell me more things about the lockbox."

"It will be better if we can get it," Pushkin said.

"You aren't going to get within a hundred miles of it," I pointed out. "If the new KGB gets a whiff of you in the country, they're coming down on you like a ton of bricks."

"Then what do you propose that we do?"

"*I* rob a bank."

Slick got back to me thirty minutes later. "You were right, Knocker. Two other things of significance. The death of an MI6 operative in Moscow and an MI5 financial terrorism officer."

"I'm going to put you on speaker so Boris can hear you."

"Roger that."

"Go ahead."

"Craig Morrow was killed just over two weeks ago in Moscow. He was supposedly meeting with someone who had intel on the upcoming British elections."

I glanced at Pushkin. "You?"

The oligarch shook his head. "No."

"Second death?"

"Teddy Allen. Looking into a company called United Holdings."

This time, Pushkin gave me a different reaction. "United Holdings is a company that funnels money into the UK for the dark operations from the Russian intelligence community."

"In this case?" I asked.

"The interference in the British elections."

"Such as?" I asked.

"Bribes, intelligence, and now, assassinations."

"All to get Pridham into power," I growled.

"It looks like it," Slick said. "By the way, those pictures. The faces belong to mercenaries who work for Stanislav Rebrov."

"Can't get away from the prick," I said.

"Listen, what do you need?" Slick asked.

"I need a team to rob a bank."

CHAPTER 6

I WAITED AS THE TEAM CLIMBED DOWN FROM THE aircraft, hauling their gear. Three men, two women. Just the people I needed to help me with what needed doing. Stuff like this was their specialty. Getting in, extracting, and getting out. They were professionals.

They were ODIN.

We were in Estonia, the perfect place to launch our operation from. I had all the intel I required and had forwarded it to ODIN team leader Ian Groves so he could formulate a plan. The man was a former SBS commander and had been running ODIN for a while now.

"Wait, are these the same people who kidnapped President Nelson?" Newman asked.

Knocker nodded. "Among other things."

"What other things?" German asked.

I cleared my throat, and they turned their attention to me rather than Knocker. I said, "The Argentinian President. Roddy Hadspen, the actor who was kidnapped in Sierra Leone. They also freed Jackie Rhodes from the Italian Mafia and Francis Jackson from the Albanians. They are professional extractors."

"Why haven't I heard about them before now?" German asked.

"Because they like to fly below the radar."

"Obviously their skills don't just relate to kidnappings."

I shook my head. *"No, far from it. They once stole a million in diamonds from a Congolese warlord, gold from a South African mercenary, and a billion dollars in bearer bonds from the North Korean President."*

"I get it, they're good."

"No," replied Knocker. *"They're the best and the only ones you want with you in a sticky situation."*

The other four were Helen Smith, Rose Holden, Paul Cross, and Evan Norris. It had been a while since I'd seen them, but they all looked to be the professionals I remembered. I took Groves's hand. "Good to see you, Ian."

"You too, Ray. You remember the rest of the team?"

"Sure do."

Groves adjusted his pack. "So, you have a curly one for us this time?"

I shook my head. "Straight forward."

"Nothing is ever straightforward," Helen Smith said.

"How about we get out of this cold weather and head to our base of operations. We can go over it there."

We climbed into two SUVs supplied by MI6. I rode with Groves. Once we were moving, he said, "You heard about the bombs in London and the other in Helsinki?"

"The Helsinki one is news to me," I replied.

"It only went off an hour or so ago. Tell me, why are we robbing a bank in St. Petersburg?"

"Because there is a lockbox there that I need to gain access to. It has papers and intel in it that are important to stopping a possible global conflict."

"Where is your partner in crime?"

"Reaper?"

"Yes."

"He's looking into some nuclear missiles."

"That bad?"

"Yeah."

Traveling for the next hour, we finally drew to a stop at a farm outside of Tallinn. We unloaded the SUVs and went inside where it was toasty warm. Stowing our kit, we headed to a large library, taking up residence in comfortable sofas and chairs around the fireplace while drinking whiskey to keep the chill out. Once settled, we started with the briefing and planning.

Groves said, "I've checked out the map and schematics of the bank. While it looks fairly straight forward, gaining access won't be the problem. Getting out is another issue. The building is situated only one block from the police station. As soon as the alarm is tripped, they'll be on the doorstep in bugger all time."

"So we don't let them trip the alarm," I said.

"Impossible. The first sign of trouble, it'll be tripped."

"Is there a way of disabling it?" I asked.

"No," Rose Holden said. "You do that, and it trips another. It's almost foolproof."

"Almost?"

"We just let them go off. Fill the street with police and army if we can."

"How are you intending to do that?"

"We're going to place a dirty big bomb on the front door for them all to see," Groves said. "Then, when the time is right, we're going to blow it up."

"You're shitting me," I said with more than a hint of uncertainty.

"Don't worry," Rose said. "It will all become clear."

"Once we explain it," Helen Smith added. "As clear as fog."

"Oh, this sounds bloody great."

She smiled at me. "It is."

"Okay, fill me in."

Groves nodded. "The first bomb won't be overly big. We want a lot of noise but not too much damage. The second bomb is the one that'll do the damage."

"Second bomb?" I asked. This was growing exponentially.

"The one we blow in the floor," Groves said. "It'll open up the sewers."

"Is that the way we're going out?" I asked.

"No," Norris said, speaking for the first time. "We're going out the front door."

"How?"

Groves said, "With all the confusion and dust that the first bomb makes, we'll go out with the hostages. Dressed as police."

"Just like that?"

The former SBS man smiled at me. "That's the plan, anyway."

"What if plan A doesn't work?" I asked.

"That's what the hole in the floor is for. First

and foremost, though, it is a diversion. It is designed to make them think that we went out that way."

I shrugged. "I'm in. I mean, what could possibly go wrong?"

Huh, what indeed?

————

St. Petersburg dawned cold the morning of the bank raid, a coating of snow having fallen late the day before. I climbed out of bed and trudged to the shower to wash and prepare for the day. Turning on the water, I waited for the shower to get as hot as I could stand it, steam billowing around the bathroom. The bank itself was only a five-minute walk from where we were staying.

I climbed into the shower and felt the water on my exposed skin. It was hot enough to prickle my skin, and the glass screen fogged up almost instantly. I started to soap my body.

Moments later, the door opened, and I felt Rose slip in behind me—

"For crying out loud, do you sleep with everyone you meet?" Holland asked, exasperated.

"I haven't slept with you."

"Must we hear of your conquests, Mr. Jensen?" Christine Ryan asked.

"If you'll give me a bloody chance, you'll realize that I wasn't about to tell you of my conquest."

"Thank God."

"You wouldn't have time to listen to them all," Knocker said with a wry smile.

I hid a grin. My friend was an acquired taste, but he was loyal and a friend for life.

"Shall we continue?"

"You have a lot of scars," Rose said to me as she took the soap and began washing my back.

"All earned the hard way," I replied.

She turned me around. The bit that stands out about her is her eyes. They were warm and caring. Not something you would see with someone who does what we do. She said, "Get out so I can finish showering."

I grinned at her and did as she bade me.

Thirty minutes later, we were ready to go. What followed next was like a scene from a movie. Five doors opened in the hotel hallway, and we all exited our rooms. We fell into line and went downstairs to the lobby where our vehicles awaited us outside.

On the way down in the elevator, I said, "Slick, you awake?"

"I'm right here, Knocker."

"Keep us updated if something changes."

"Roger that."

We went out into the parking lot and climbed into the SUVs. There was still some snow on the ground from the previous day. With Groves leading the way, we parked a block away from the bank and grabbed our bags. Following the sidewalk until we reached a point close to the front door, we stopped, put on our masks, and went inside.

Groves and Norris entered first, both armed with HT420s. These were handguns that looked like your average weapon but fired an electronically charged round. A lot like a taser but without the wires.

As they went through the second door, Groves moved right, and Norris left. There were two guards. They shot them both and the electrical charge hit them like a horse's kick. The guards fell and remained still.

Cross, me, and Rose came in next. We were armed with the real deal. Glocks and MP7s. Helen stopped on the way in and set the explosive charge. Meanwhile, the silent alarm had been tripped and we were rounding up staff and customers.

"Get them along the windows," Groves called out. "Find me the manager."

We worked on organizing the handful of customers and staff into rows against the panes of glass while Norris went to locate the bank's manager. A thin man in a gray suit was soon brought before Groves. "Are you the manager?" he asked in Russian.

"Yes."

"Good, take me to the safety deposit boxes."

"What?"

Groves pressed the 420 against his forehead. "Don't fuck with me."

The manager led the way, and I followed them. Rose kept an eye on the prisoners while Helen kept watch. Norris and Cross set the charge to blow a hole in the floor in a back room. We'd only just entered the safe deposit room when Helen said, "The first police cars are pulling up now, boss."

"Copy." He shoved the manager. "Seven six two."

The manager looked back at the former SBS man.

"You fucking heard me. Seven six two."

The manager edged along the wall of boxes until he reached the one we wanted. "Th-this one."

"Open it."

"I do not have a key."

"Fuck off, I know you have a master key. Now open it."

The man nodded and fumbled with something in his pocket. His hand emerged with a key, and he put it into the box, turned, and pulled it out.

"Stand back," I snapped.

He took a step back and I pulled the box the rest of the way. I placed it on the nearby table and opened the lid. It was full of papers. I emptied the metal box, placing the contents into a backpack.

"We're good here," I said.

"Okay," Groves said and shot the manager with one of the shock rounds. The middle-aged man fell to the floor, unconscious. "Let's get ready."

From outside, the first attempt at contact was made. A bullhorn was used. When we emerged into the main reception area, Helen turned and said, "They want to talk to someone."

Groves nodded. "Let's see what they want. Make sure everything is ready to go."

He walked to the door and opened it a crack. "What do you want?" he asked in Russian.

"We want you to surrender. There is nothing else you can do."

"What if I don't want to?"

"What other choice do you have?"

Groves looked around and saw armed officers taking up strategic positions. He guessed that there were snipers on the rooftops as well. "I want a bus and a plane ready to go."

"We cannot do that," the metallic voice replied.

"Then you leave me no choice."

"What do you mean?"

"You'll see."

Groves started to close the door. "Wait."

He stopped. "We need time."

"Fine, you've got an hour."

The door closed and Groves walked over to us. In a low voice, he said, "They won't wait that long. Get them away from the windows, get the other charges in place, and then change clothes."

"Slick, tell me what you're seeing out there," I said into my comms.

"There are more and more police arriving all the time. It looks like they've got an armored car and their version of a SWAT team."

"Love it," I said. "If this goes wrong, we're fucked."

"Pretty much."

The hostages were moved into a back room out of harm's way. Once they were secured, we all changed into our police clothing. I said, "I'm glad they don't have new uniforms."

Norris said, "There was a time when we tried this in Rio."

"That obviously worked," I replied.

"Nope, I can't say that it did."

"Oh, great."

"They had different uniforms," Rose said. "We changed the plan on the run. We got out, but only just."

"Does everyone have their smoke grenades?" Groves asked.

"Yes, boss."

"Good, when I give the word, pull the pins and

throw them around."

We waited for the next forty-five minutes while the police and the armed forces outside got set up.

"Looks like they're about ready to move," Slick said to me.

"All right, let Groves know."

He relayed the message, and Groves said, "All right, positions. Let's do this."

We all put on our gas masks and got ready. Moments later, the countdown began. "Three…two…one…execute."

The blasts sounded as one. The hole in the floor opened up, and the windows and front door went. Next, we pulled the pins on the smoke grenades and let them go. Soon, the bank was filled with smoke.

I heard Groves say, "Any movement?"

"They're on their way."

"Okay, bring them out and get the flashbangs ready."

Moments later, as the police were entering, we had the civilians out in the main area and Norris and Helen dropped two flashbangs.

Their detonations were the signal for the chaos to begin. We started shouting at the hostages to move toward the doors. Though disoriented, they managed to move in that direction. The bank was a mix of civilians and police, and we were blending in. Soon, we had the hostages outside and hurrying away from the front of the bank.

I could hear the reports starting to come over the radio that they'd found a hole in the floor and that they needed more people inside. It was in this chaos that we slipped away and disappeared. The plan had worked.

———

We all gathered in my hotel room and started to go through the papers and contents of the lockbox. For two hours, we each pored over the documents, and it was Rose who finally made the breakthrough. "Denis Sobolev."

"He's Pridham's grandfather. We knew that."

"What about Max Stiles?"

"Okay, I'll bite. Who is Max Stiles?"

"Max Stiles was former MI6. He was disavowed a few years back and went over to the Russians as some kind of fixer."

"What kind of fixer?" I wanted to know.

"He did dirty work for them. Like an assassin but he also got things that needed to be got."

"What does he have to do with this?"

"I don't know?"

I nodded. "Then I need to find out."

Grabbing my cell, I dialed a familiar number and waited. "You have the keyboard king."

"Slick, I need to know where Max Stiles is and what he's doing?"

"What Max Stiles might that be?" he asked.

"The one who used to work for MI6. He's changed sides and is working for the Russians."

"I'll see what I can do."

Groves smiled. "I guess that's it. We are done here."

I fixed my gaze on the former SBS commander. "Thanks for your help, Ian."

"My pleasure. I hope you get what you need."

"Where to for you now?" I asked him.

"Australia. It seems some crime family down there have stolen vital intel from the government and they need someone to get it back."

"Good luck."

"You, too."

Groves and his people left, and I set about waiting for news from Slick. Two hours later, Mr. Reliable got back to me. "Max Stiles was last seen boarding a flight to Belarus from Berlin."

"Do you know why?"

"Not a clue," Slick replied. "He was keeping company with Andreas Seeler. He's—"

"I know who he is," I said.

"Then you also know what he does."

"Yes. Shit. Get me a ride to Berlin, Slick, I need to talk to Seeler."

"On it."

The call disconnected and I stared at the picture of Seeler. He was an arms dealer I'd crossed paths with on more than one occasion. My attention went back to the papers. Most of which confirmed things I already knew. However, Stiles was in it for a reason. I just needed to know what that was and how he fitted in. The only way to get that answer was from the man himself. I was still staring at his picture when my locked and secure room door snicked open.

I turned and brought my Glock up, my finger firm on the trigger. "Hello, Raymond."

"Hello, Natalia."

Natalia Kochneva. I hadn't seen her since my last visit to Mali. On that occasion, she was trying to kill me for blowing her operation wide open. Now, she was standing in front of me. Her long dark hair hung past her slender shoulders, her dark smoldering eyes questioning my presence in St. Petersburg.

Surprisingly, she didn't have a gun.

Closing the door, she turned back to face me. "Why are you here, Raymond?"

"How did you know I was?" I asked her.

"I saw you enter the hotel with the others," she replied.

I nodded slowly. "I had something to do, and now it's time to leave. How is life in the new KGB?"

She shrugged noncommittally. "It is so-so."

"Just so-so?"

"Uh, huh."

I stared at her. "Why are you here, Natalia?"

"Yury Gazinsky."

Now I was on edge. "What about him?"

"I know he is dead, and I know you were with him," she replied.

"I didn't kill him, though."

"I know. It was them."

"By them, I take it you mean Rebrov and his mercenaries."

"Yes. Yury was my friend. Now they must pay. I want to know why they did it."

"Because he was meeting me and they didn't like that," I replied.

"Why?"

I thought about it and then nodded. "What the fuck."

What followed next was me giving her a rundown on pretty much everything. When I finished, Natalia stared at me in disbelief. "You expect me to believe that Lash is trying to start a war to take back the lands he claims belong to the USSR?"

I shrugged. "Quite frankly, I don't give a bugger if you believe me or not. That's what is happening. My friend is trying to get to their missiles before they can use them. We already took one lot out. A couple of their generals are already dead, and Shatov is still pressing forward with the crazy plan that he, Lash, and the other generals came up with."

"That is why Yury died?"

"Yury died because he was trying to help me and because he was friends with Boris Pushkin."

"Pushkin is a traitor," she spat. "Yury would never become involved with him."

"Boris was no traitor," I told her. I grabbed the papers I'd been looking through. "Here."

For the next twenty minutes, she perused the intel in silence. When Natalia was finished, she looked up at me and said, "What are you going to do?"

"I have to go to Berlin. I need to see Andreas Seeler and ask him about Max Stiles."

There was no hesitation in her response. "I will come with you."

"Why?" I looked at her, not certain of her motives.

"For Yury."

I nodded. "Fine, but you follow orders."

"We will see."

CHAPTER 7

BERLIN WAS OVER THE BLIZZARD THAT HAD SHUT THE CITY down, and things were now almost back to normal. Normal for winter that is.

After landing and getting out of the airport, we headed for an MI6 safe house, arriving and grabbing our bags—

"You took a foreign agent to one of our safehouses?" German asked.

I watched as Knocker nodded. "Sure did."

"Are you insane?"

He shook his head. "You don't have to concern yourself about it."

"Why not?"

"It doesn't exist anymore."

"I'm not surprised after you took the woman there. MI6 would have to shut it down immediately."

"No," Knocker replied.

"What do you mean?"

"I blew it up."

I couldn't help myself and laughed out loud. I saw

Newman smile, the same as Holly. After that moment of
brevity, Knocker continued.

The safehouse was on the outskirts of Berlin. We
set up there and I made a few calls to some old friends.
The intel they provided allowed me to move to the
next stage of my operation. The call disconnected and
Natalia asked, "Where is Seeler?"

"We're in luck," I replied. "Tonight, he is dining
with Cobalt Murphy."

"That man is a fucking lunatic," she almost spat the
words.

"So am I, my love."

"Don't call me that."

"Sorry. Too much Open All Hours."

"I know what it is," she replied.

"Good thing they've got more than one bed then,
isn't it?"

"Where is Seeler?"

"A place in East Berlin frequented by an insalu-
brious lot," I replied.

"Of course. What is the plan?"

"We go and ask nicely."

Natalia raised her eyebrows. "Nicely?"

"Really nicely."

She stared at me and then shook her head. "Shit."

———

It is amazing how many places an MP7 will get you
into. You just walk up to the door, flash it from under
your long coat, and the security ushers you right in.
Now, in a place like this, there was no need to worry
about the loss of innocent lives.

Every person here was a criminal. Either wanted by local law, Interpol, or some other country's law enforcement, many on most wanted lists. Two I knew immediately. One was an American responsible for trafficking women from his own country to Europe—though not anymore. Once we'd left there, I let my friends on the Talon team know that he was about. The other was a Belgian known to smuggle ecstasy throughout Europe.

Eyes were immediately drawn to us. Strangers were regarded as dangers. Ha, did you see what I did there? Anyway, among the clientele, we were threats, which set most of them on edge.

A woman walked past with a tray of drinks. She was wearing a short skirt and a low-cut top, her breasts billowing upward. Outside, she would have frozen, but in here, I was beginning to think that the less clothing one wore, the better.

I reached out and grabbed a glass of brown fluid. I took a sip. It was scotch, so I knocked the rest of it back before placing the empty glass on the tray, giving the waitress a wink.

"Are you done?" Natalia asked me.

I nodded at the second glass. "You should try it. The stuff is good."

So she did. "You are right."

The music in the club was not what I had expected. A gifted pianist accompanied a female soloist singing sultry jazz, her voice redolent of a sixty-cigarette-a-day habit. It was low and husky but sexy at the same time.

We were shown to the table where Seeler was seated with Cobalt Murphy and two other men. Seeler stared at us, unfamiliar with our identity. Murphy, on the other hand, knew exactly who I was. "Ray Jensen, what the fuck do you want?"

His accent was heavy Irish. "Hello, Cobalt. You out shopping?"

His red-bearded face screwed up in what appeared to be anger, or it might have been normal for the crazy motherfucker. "What the fuck does it have to do with you?"

I shook my head. "Nothing. I'm here to see Seeler, actually."

Natalia moved a few feet away from me, guarding my flank.

The arms dealer stared at me. "Who are you?"

"Ray Jensen. My friends call me—"

"Cunt," Murphy snarled.

"Now, Cobalt, that's not very pleasant. Think of the ladies present."

"What fucking ladies?" I cast a glance at Natalia. He said, "All I see is a fucking whore."

"Can I shoot him, Raymond?" she asked.

"And a Russian whore at that," Murphy added.

"Not just yet, Natalia. Maybe once we've concluded our business."

An explosion was bubbling just beneath Murphy's surface, and I knew we'd be lucky to get out of there without killing him. As they say, you should eliminate threats before they eliminate you. "Shit. Okay, Natalia."

A P-96 handgun appeared in her hand and cracked. And she shot him.

The Irishman's head snapped back, and he slumped in the seat. Immediately, people were moving, and guns came out. Beneath my coat, I brought my twin MP7s to join the party. Moments later, I was standing there like Chuck Norris on the movie poster for Invasion USA.

"Let's think about this before someone does something stupid."

The tense atmosphere crackled throughout the club until Seeler raised his hand and the weapons went away. I said to him, "You got somewhere we can talk in private?"

Suddenly, a skinny man appeared, raging about one of his customers being shot. He was flanked by two big thugs who were armed. I rolled my eyes and shoved the barrel of an MP7 under his chin. "Fuck off, I'm busy."

He glanced at Seeler. The arms dealer said, "Can we use your office, Johann?"

The man nodded.

Natalia and I followed Seeler down a long corridor to the manager's office. When the door was closed with Natalia standing guard, Seeler said, "Now, why have you fucked up my night?"

"Max Stiles," I said.

"What about him?"

"He was here visiting you. He's gone to Belarus. I need to know where and what for," I informed him.

"I do not know," Seeler lied.

"You know what he wanted," I pointed out. "One just doesn't meet with an arms dealer to say hi. What did he want?"

Seeler hesitated. "You are asking me to break the confidence of a customer."

"If you see it that way. I wouldn't do that. After all, a businessman's word is like a binding contract."

"That's right."

"Natalia, on the other hand, works for the KGB. They don't give a fuck about such principles. If you don't give us what we need, then she will kill you."

He was growing nervous, glanced at Natalia, then back at me. "You will ruin me."

"We won't breathe a word. And I doubt that you will say anything either."

"He—he came looking for automated miniguns."

"Why?"

Seeler shook his head. "I don't know. He said he needed them for a job."

"Why Belarus?"

"There is a man there who can help," the arms dealer said.

"Who?"

"Viktor," Natalia said in a low voice.

Seeler nodded. "Yes."

"Who is Viktor?" I asked.

"Viktor Suvorov. Former Russian general who is selling the weapons that he steals from across the world. Is he having a garage sale?"

"Yes."

"When?"

"Tomorrow night."

"Where?"

Seeler shook his head. "I don't know. You need to be invited."

"Can you get us invited?" I asked, giving him a look that communicated the gravity of my request.

"No! No, I couldn't do that."

"But you can," I said.

"It would be possible, but I could not do it."

Natalia closed the gap between them and placed her handgun against his head. "I do not think you have a choice."

Stammering as he fumbled with his cell, he made the call, and ten minutes later, we had our invitation.

Exiting the club through the rear door, I called Holly. "We need a ride to Belarus."

"When?"

"Tonight."

"Go back to the safehouse. I'll send someone for you."

———

She did, but they were too late. Seeler, incensed that he had been humiliated in front of his people, was unprepared to let our little chat go and sent a team after us. As with most criminal enterprises, their intel was better than law enforcement. If you ever need to know about a hard-to-find someone, just go to the wrong side of the law.

The only reason we had any notion they were coming was the motion sensors. A warning was triggered on the screens, and we could see them advancing. Without hesitation, I said to Natalia, "Get ready to leave."

"What are you going to do?"

"Leave a surprise."

I went into the saferoom and hit a switch, which gave us only a minute to leave. After that, if we were still in the house, we would be spread all over the landscape and they'd be picking us up for a week.

I scooped up an MP7 and headed for the back door. Natalia was waiting for me. "You ready?"

"Yes."

"Let's do this."

We burst out through the rear door and ran across the backyard. These guys were amateurs. Their plan was obviously to enter the house through the front door without sending anyone to cover the back. Their mistake.

They entered and died. The house blew big and loud. Anyone who went inside failed to come out.

————

Minsk wasn't the place to be. Russian soldiers were visible on the streets with the local armed forces as the tensions grew with the West. The build-up along the border with Poland was strengthening every day.

Arriving early in the morning, we were met at the airport by an SUV, and I drove us into the city to locate another old friend. This one was a thief. Nothing more, just a thief who had set up a network over the years, gathering intel like picking up rocks from the street.

"What is his name?" Natalia asked me.

"Some bloody thing I can't pronounce," I replied. "So, I just call him Ricky."

"And where is this Ricky?"

"You wouldn't believe it if I told you. Just wait, you'll see."

Ten minutes later, I pulled into a McDonald's parking lot. Natalia glanced at me and said, "You are kidding?"

"I shit you not."

Parking the SUV, we climbed out and walked to the fast-food giant's entry door. Pushing through the smudged glass, I looked around, spotting Ricky in a booth toward the rear. His hair was long, his face unshaven. Seated across the table from him were two men. We walked through the tables toward the back, and when we stopped at the second to last booth, he looked up at me.

"Hello, Ricky."

"Ray Jensen," he said with a wry grin. "Fuck off."

"I need your help, Ricky. It'll only take a minute."

"No."

"There's ten grand in it for you."

He looked at the men across from him. "Go."

The pair rose and left. The power of money. Ricky stared at the computer in front of him while we sat down. I said, "Got something going on, Ricky?"

"Art theft in Paris."

"Big job?"

"Three million."

"Big enough."

"And they let you operate your business out of here?" Natalia asked.

Ricky glanced at her and then at me. "Who is she?"

"Natalia Kochneva. KGB."

Ricky nodded. "I heard they'd gone back to the old days."

"Heard?" I asked. "Where the fuck have you been? The Russians have all but taken over your country."

"They like to think it's theirs. They've been here so long I've forgotten what it used to be like." He looked at Natalia. "And, to answer your question, I own this place."

"Okay."

Ricky stared at me. "Why are you working with a woman from the KGB?"

"Actually, she is considering her options."

He perked up. "Really. I could use someone with your talents. Pays well. Twenty-thousand US."

Natalia's eyebrows shot up. "Twenty thousand a year? No thanks."

"No, twenty a month."

I shook my head. "Christ, Ricky, business must be good."

"Never been better. Now, Raymond, what do you want?"

"Max Stiles," I replied.

"What about him?"

"He's in town meeting up with Viktor Suvorov. I need to know where."

"I might have heard something," he replied. "I'll need to make a call to confirm it. Get yourself a Big Mac while you wait."

I did as he suggested and sat down across from Natalia in a different booth. I drank some Coke and took a bite of the burger before spitting it out into the bag it came from. "No wonder he's still a thief."

I settled on the Coke. Natalia knew better than to pollute her body with the stuff served up here but had bought a bottle of water. "How do you know this man?"

"I met him sometime back when I was on a job for MI6. A weapons dealer had acquired some nerve agent. I was given Ricky's name as the man who'd stolen it."

"Did he?"

"Yes. Only he didn't know what it was. He helped me track down the seller and buyer. We've been associates ever since."

"Not friends?"

"Fuck, no."

A few minutes later, Ricky joined us. He looked at me and said, "Money?"

I stared back.

His shoulders slumped. "I just knew you were fucking me over."

"Come on, Ricky. I let you stay in business, shouldn't that be enough?"

"Screw you, Ray," he snapped.

"What do you have?"

He looked at Natalia. "Can you believe this?"

She nodded. "Yes, he screwed me once too."

"Really?"

"Yes, it lasted all of thirty seconds."

"Oh." He frowned, the dime suddenly dropping. "Oh, oh."

"If you two are finished," I said, "can we get back to matters at hand?"

"Was she too much woman for you, Ray? I can see why."

"You stupid dick," I growled. "What she means is I fucked her over—"

"Yes," Natalia said, interrupting. "Over a barrel. It was exciting."

"Christ. I blew her operation apart in Mali."

"Not the only thing that was blown," she shot back.

"Not bloody helping, Natalia."

She shrugged and smiled. "It is fun."

"What do you have, Ricky?" I asked again.

"Max Stiles has a meeting this evening with Suvorov," he replied.

"No shit. I already knew that."

"It will be on the outskirts of Minsk at the new industrial building site."

"Okay. What is he buying?"

"Automated miniguns."

I nodded. "That checks out."

"Yes, but they are mobile. Mounted in two vans. All you have to do is park them and forget they're there."

This wasn't good and I wasn't liking what I was hearing. "They can be remotely operated?" I asked.

"Yes. Even the door slides open of its own accord."

"So, it could be sat anywhere, and the person operating it could be anywhere."

Ricky nodded. "That's about it."

I stood up. "Thanks, Ricky."

"You could do that by paying me," he replied.

"Thanks, Ricky."

―――――

The industrial estate site covered five acres with buildings in various stages of construction. There were pallets and stacks of building materials scattered everywhere, but I figured the buy would take place somewhere closer to the center of the construction area. There was a vacant allotment out of sight, surrounded by half-built warehouses.

We set ourselves up on the second floor of one such building, overlooking the area we expected the exchange to take place. Natalia and I were armed with HK 433 11-inch.

"How do you know they will be here?" Natalia asked.

"Just an informed guess."

"In other words, they could be anywhere," she shot back at me.

I had no answer for that. "Slick, anything?"

"Nothing yet, Knocker."

I looked at my watch. We'd been there for a while. Maybe too long, and I was starting to think that the buy was going down elsewhere. Then headlights appeared.

"Knocker, we've got movement," Slick said from the comfort of the MI6 operations room.

"I've got them, Slick. Looks to be two SUVs. No, looks to be an SUV and a van. This could be the seller."

We remained silent as the vehicles approached. They stopped right where I guessed they would. I said, "Bingo. All we need now is the buyer."

Moments later, another SUV appeared and stopped in the headlights of the other vehicles. Two men climbed out. One was Max Stiles, the other I'd never seen before. They talked for several moments, and then I saw Suvorov indicate toward the van. The door slid open, and I saw the mounted minigun sitting there like a cobra, ready to strike.

CHAPTER 8

"THIS IS GOING TO BE INTERESTING," I SAID TO NATALIA.

"How does it work?" she asked. "Have you seen them before?"

"Yes. They have sensors with the ability to track targets. Any movement is detected and tracked, firing until the target is down."

"It looks like we're about to get a demonstration."

People started to move back except for one man. He was the one who had arrived with Stiles. I raised my weapon to get a better view through optics. The man looked relaxed. Suvorov spoke briefly to him, and the man started to jump left and right. I changed the direction I was looking, over to the van and saw the minigun tracking his movements. Glancing at Natalia, I could see she was doing the same.

Then things changed. The man stopped and Suvorov directed one of his men to the van. He climbed in and started to fiddle with the minigun. Once he was done, he gave his boss the thumbs up.

"What are they doing?" Natalia asked.

"Live fire test," I replied grimly.

"On what?"

Her question was answered by the sudden movement of the live target. This time, it was more frantic and desperate. Suddenly, the tracking minigun opened fire, its blazing, rotating barrels emitting flame and tracer. The first frenetic blast missed, but only just, the next didn't. The target seemed to disintegrate before our eyes.

"Fucking hell," I groaned.

"What now?" Natalia asked.

"Now I've seen enough."

My 433 sights came to rest on Suvorov. Looking back, it was probably the wrong move. I stroked the trigger, and the round hurtling from the weapon's barrel punched into his chest.

The arms dealer fell to the ground, his life gone. Beside me, Natalia opened fire and another thug fell beside the dead man. Everyone began to scatter, except for the guy operating the minigun. He was about the only one who was cool under fire. He located us and set the devastating weapon alight.

Everything around us began to erupt under the overwhelming incoming fire. Our world was torn apart, and all we could do was hug the floor we were on and hope for the best.

"Great fucking plan, Raymond," Natalia shouted at me.

"Don't fucking call me Raymond!"

"Well, what—" She stopped as rounds just missed. "What now, you fucking genius?"

I started shoving myself backward. "Follow me."

"Where to?"

"Anywhere but here."

The minigun totally destroyed the front of the semi-built structure. Once it had lost its fix, it sprayed the whole building erratically. Natalia and I made our way down to the ground and around the side of a separate building where we could get a fix on the van. However, it was too late. By the time we were in position, the firing had stopped and the van was pulling away.

"Slick, we've lost the target."

"Roger. I'll see if I can pick him up."

"Come on, Natalia, let's go."

She shook her head. "Leave me. I might have a way of finding out where Stiles is going."

"No, Slick will find him," I assured her.

"Two heads are better than one," she said with a smile. "Isn't that what you Englishmen say?"

"Something like that."

"I will come to you in the morning."

"I'll meet you at Ricky's. About seven."

"I will be there."

Then she left. I never saw her—

"You gave her information and let her get away from you?" Holland blurted out. *"Bloody typical. You have to be the most unprofessional —"*

"Shut the fuck up," I said, backing Knocker.

"Pardon?"

"You heard. If you had let him finish, you would have known that he was about to say that it was the last time he saw Natalia alive."

He stared at me, then at Knocker. Then he shut up.

The next morning, I got a call from Slick telling me that he'd tracked the van but then lost it in a tunnel.

They had to have switched vehicles. The problem was, they were prepared. Five vans left the tunnel at the same time. Then they disappeared.

"Is there any possible way to locate him?"

"He has a female friend in Antwerp. She might be the one to ask."

"Fine, get me and Natalia a flight."

"Roger that."

———

Arriving at Ricky's McDonald's was something I won't forget for a while. Everything was quiet when I got there. The parking lot was empty except for two SUVs. I climbed from the vehicle I was in and walked toward the building in the cold morning air.

Even as I touched the door to push it open, the silence hit me, and I knew that something was wrong. The first body I saw on the floor was one of Ricky's men. He'd been shot twice in the chest, once in the head. The killing had been professional.

The Glock came out of my pants, and I raised it, sweeping the restaurant ahead of me. Ricky was sitting in his booth, slumped to one side, his computer open, blood splattered on the window behind him.

I glanced around, looking for Natalia. At first, I didn't see her. But as I walked past the next booth, she was there, lying on the floor, slumped under the table. She'd been shot four times. Once in the shoulder, another in the leg, and then again in the head and chest.

"Slick, I have a problem."

"Go ahead, Knocker."

"They're all dead. I need you to try to hook into their CCTV."

"Roger that."

I continued clearing the room, including the restrooms. Moving into the kitchen area where the food was cooked and prepared, there was no trace of anyone, including staff. I went back out into the restaurant. "Talk to me, Slick."

"It appears things went down about an hour ago," he said. "Looks like a team of four shooters burst in and killed them all. They never knew what hit them."

"How the hell did they know?"

"This looks interesting," Slick replied.

"What?"

"Sending it to your phone."

The incoming message notification pinged, and I withdrew it from my pocket, punching in the unlock code. Moments later, I was watching a video feed. The assailants arrived on site, pushing Natalia ahead of them. When the shooting started, she dived off to the side. But it wasn't Ricky or his friend who shot her, it was the people she had arrived with. "She was their prisoner," I said.

"It looks that way."

"Fuck. Find out who they are."

As I continued to watch the video, another man appeared. He looked to be older, maybe in his sixties. "Slick, are you seeing this?"

"Roger that."

"Any idea who he is?" I asked.

"Give me a moment, Knocker."

Returning to the last booth, I stared down at Natalia's mortal remains. If she had any information to give to me, it had died with her. "All right," Slick said. "I have a name. Oleg Zhirkov. Former Russian general supposedly died in a plane crash over Ukraine."

"He's the missing general," I said.

"It would seem so."

"Why is he here?"

"My guess is that he was triggered when Natalia started making inquiries."

He was right. It wouldn't take much. Then all they had to do was find her. "Any idea where they went from here?"

"Nothing. They used their usual trick and shut everything down."

"Then why not here?" I asked.

"Maybe they wanted you to know it was them," Slick said.

"Well, if that's the case, they have their wish. And God fucking help them when I get hold of him. Time to go to Antwerp."

―――――

The woman in Antwerp I needed to see was Mary McKillop, a native of England, like Max Stiles. Slick had me on a flight within hours, and two hours after that, I was in Antwerp and ready to question the woman. A resident of one of the more affluent regions of the city, I could only assume that the fortune amassed by Stiles went back to her, and she lived the high life while he roamed the world selling weapons.

I figured he was bound to come home every now and again, but not as often as she liked. How do I know that? It might have had something to do with the young man leaving her premises that morning when I arrived across the street. She gave him a passionate farewell just inside the front door with it open.

After he had disappeared, I climbed from my vehicle and hurried across the wet pavement. I rang the doorbell and waited. Moments later, she answered, giving me a questioning look. "Mary McKillop?"

She frowned at me. "Yes."

"My name is Ray Jensen. I need to ask you a few questions, if that's okay?"

"What about?"

"Max Stiles."

"I'm sorry I have nothing to say to you." She began backing away and started closing the door.

While on the flight to Antwerp, I had taken the time to peruse a file sent to me by Slick. Apparently, Mary MacKillop was former MI6 as well. When Stiles had been disavowed, she'd left the Security Service. Now, of all things, she was a security adviser with a company based in the city. According to her bank details, she earned a healthy £700,000 per year. She also had a son. His name was Gregory.

Speaking through the rapidly narrowing gap, I called to her, "It would be in your best interest, Mary, to talk to me. I'm from MI6, and what I have to say is best for you to hear." I gave her my most disarming smile and hoped it would work.

She hesitated and then opened the door again, stepping aside to allow me to pass. "Okay, I'll hear what you have to say."

Once the door was closed behind us, she showed me through to a large and comfortable living room.

She gestured with a hand, and I sat down. "Would you like a drink?"

"What are you offering?" I asked her.

"Coffee or scotch."

"I'll take the coffee, thanks."

A few minutes later, she was back with a tray holding coffee cups, setting it on the dark wood coffee table in front of us. As she passed me a cup, she asked, "What is it you want to know about Max?"

"Do you know where he is?"

"No idea," she lied.

"Are you sure, Mary?"

"I just said so, didn't I?" Her voice was snippy.

"I think you're lying," I replied. "In fact, I think you know where he's going and what he's up to."

"Then you would be wrong."

"How's Gregory, Mary?"

Her eyes flickered.

I continued. "You see, I've just come from Belarus. Max was buying some automatic miniguns. Nasty fucking weapons they are. I think he's working for the Russians. It's a wild guess, but I think I'm right."

She shrugged and shook her head. "I wouldn't know."

"There it is. You're lying to me again. For a woman who worked with MI6, you are not very good at it. Now, we can do this the easy way or the hard way. And I'm sure you know what the hard way is."

"Fuck you, asshole."

"Now your true colors are starting to show. All you have to do is tell me where Max is. Nothing too hard."

"And if I don't?" Mary asked.

"I already told you, Mary. First, we get the information out of you and then we send you away into a deep dark hole for a very long time. How do you think Gregory will like that? I can tell you right now he will never see his mother again."

If there's one thing you can always count on, it's a mother's love for their offspring. Even the threat of never seeing them again was enough. "He was going back to England."

"How? Where? When?"

She shook her head. "I don't know. He said it was something big."

"It's big all right."

I heard the slam of vehicle doors coming from the front of her home. I rose from the sofa, crossed to the window, and peered out. There was a black SUV parked out the front. Four men had just got out of it and were coming up the path. I turned to Mary and said, "Who did you call?"

"No one."

"Then why are there four men coming up your path?"

"I don't know."

"Shit, out the back."

"I'm not going anywhere with you."

"Fine, I don't give a shit. Have it your way."

I hurried back to the hallway, intending to use it to access the back door of the house. I hadn't gone far when the front door blew in. It came away from the hinges and flew six feet inward before hitting me. I fell forward, my head hitting hard.

My head was swimming, my thoughts making no sense at all. I moaned and rolled onto my back. The ceiling above me seemed to spin, and a face loomed over me. It took me a moment to work out who it was. Mary.

She said, "You made a mistake the moment you threatened me, Mr. Jensen."

Then darkness claimed me, and I remembered nothing until I woke up two hours later.

———

The little men banging away with their hammers inside my head were having a merry old time when I woke up. My arms were sore, and I couldn't work out why until I realized they were chained above my head, and I was hanging there, my feet barely able to touch the hard concrete floor.

"Well, well, you're awake."

The voice was male, gruff. British. My eyes opened and took a while to focus, but there he was, sitting on a chair some ten feet away from me in the middle of what looked to be an empty warehouse.

"I'm beginning to wish I wasn't," I replied. "My fucking head hurts."

"Yeah, getting swiped by a door will do that, Jensen."

Finally, my eyes focused. He was a solid man with dark hair, and wearing warm clothing. He held a handgun pointed at the floor. "You seem to have me at a disadvantage."

"The name is Croft. Elias Croft."

The computer hard drive in my head started flicking through files automatically. Elias Croft, Elias Croft... "Yeah, I got you. Former Para Captain. Got kicked out for murdering civilians."

"They weren't murdered. They were enemy combatants."

"I guess someone else saw things the other way. Now I guess you're doing mercenary work while trying to stay one step ahead of the law."

"It pays better than the paras."

I coughed as pain shot through my shoulders. "So, what now?"

"We'll see."

A few minutes later, Mary appeared flanked by two of Croft's men. A picture began to form in my head. She was part of it somehow. Coming to stand in front of me, she was dressed differently, wearing a red dress and a long fur coat. "Going out, Mary?"

Her smile matched the weather outside. "Business meeting followed by dinner with a client."

"The same one you fucked last night?"

Mary stepped in close and slapped my face. Hard, drawing blood. It trickled from my split lip. She stared at it without saying a word, smiled, then stepped closer and licked it off.

"Is that all I get? How about you kiss it better?"

The smile on her face grew larger. "Next you'll be wanting me to suck your cock, Ray."

"Well, if you're granting final wishes…"

She reached up and tore my shirt open. Somewhere along the way, my coat had been removed. It exposed my hairy chest and the many battle scars I'd collected over the years. She stepped back, admiring the sight, wanting to touch it—

"Mr. Jensen," Christine Ryan said with more than a hint of doubt in her voice.

Knocker shrugged. "Well, she could have."

"Stick to the facts."

She stepped back, staring at my exposed chest. "Raymond—"

"You don't get to call me Raymond. Not unless you're going to sleep with me."

"Raymond, why are you after Max?"

"I need to find out if he's busy tomorrow night. I guess he's out of town, though, especially if his squeeze is sleeping with some other guy. Who was he, anyway?"

She smiled. "Someone whose name you will never know."

"You don't do other women as well, do you?" I asked her. "Maybe we could come to some arrangement."

There was a rattling noise, and I looked up to see another guy wheeling a small trolley with a power pack on it. "Ah, fuck, don't you criminal types have any new ideas on how to torture a man. Shit."

A couple of minutes later, I was hooked up and waiting, my anticipation unbridled for the juice to start flowing. "Before you start, can you take my pants off?"

Mary frowned at me. "Why would we do that?"

"I've been zapped before, and the first thing that's going to happen is I'm going to piss myself. I'd rather not do that with my pants on. Tends to smell."

Mary nodded at one of her men. He took a step forward. Shaking my head, I said, "No, you do it. My worst nightmare is getting undressed by a guy."

"Are you trying to waste my time, Mr. Jensen?"

I winked at her. "It shows, huh?"

"Get started."

"No, wait, I was serious about the pants."

Her man took them off. I was thankful for that because the first jolt from the power pack made me piss everywhere. Only because I was busting to go in the first place. When the torturer released the paddles, my muscles relaxed, and my cries of pain stopped. Mary nodded to the puddle on the floor. "You were right, you did piss yourself."

"I hate being right," I replied.

"Hit him again."

Fire shot through my body, along with excruciating pain. My muscles contracted until I thought they would explode, and I almost passed out. Then it stopped and my head sagged to my chest. It brought back memories of Turkey, except they were using more juice.

"Now, Mr. Jensen, why are you after Max?"

I mumbled something incoherent.

"What was that?"

My head came up. "He got my sister pregnant."

"Again."

This time, I did pass out.

I think I was out for only a few minutes before they used water to bring me around. I coughed and spluttered, and my head jerked up from the shock of the cold liquid. Mary was still there. "Now, Mr. Jensen, what have you got to tell me?"

"That fucking hurts."

"You can stop the pain, just tell me what I want to know."

It would have been easy to just give in, but I'm not the quitting type. Actually, I haven't been accused of being smart much either. "Don't you have a meeting to go to?"

I passed out again. This time, it was for longer because when they finally woke me up, I was lying on the floor, and Mary was gone.

Rolling over, I stared up at the ceiling of the warehouse. The floor was freezing, and I could feel the warmth draining rapidly from my body. "Hello, Ray, back in the land of the living?"

"You still here, Croft, I thought you might have gone with your fucking psycho boss."

He shrugged. "She still wants answers."

"So, what's next?"

"We might try something different."

Croft and his men pulled me to my feet before forcing me into a chair where they tied me good and tight. When I was secured, they placed a leather strap around my forehead, fastening it to the back of the chair. Then Croft reached into his pocket and took out a set of extraction forceps utilized by dentists.

"Really, we're going to go there?" I asked.

The mercenary shrugged. "You were given the chance."

Then he took out one of my teeth. Not one from the front. They're too easy. He went for a molar. When he started, I think I preferred being electrocuted. The forceps clamped on my tooth, and I could hear them crunch and feel them grate against it. Then he started to pull, and it felt like half of my head was coming away with it.

I screamed. I don't mind admitting it. It bloody hurt. Then the pressure was released, and with a flood of blood, the tooth came free.

Tears rolled down my cheeks from the pain. Croft held the bloody tooth up in front of my face and said, "Wow, that was a big one. I bet it hurt."

"Fuck you." I spat blood from my mouth, and it landed on my chest.

Croft smiled. "I'll give you a minute to prepare."

I don't think anyone could prepare for that shit. It was a case of riding the pain until you couldn't deal with it anymore. Maybe I'd get lucky and pass out as he extracted the next one.

Somehow, I think the waiting was the worst. Maybe getting it over and done with would have been better. Then he came back with his friends and prepared to take out the next tooth.

He leaned in. "Are you ready, Raymond?"

Suddenly, Croft's head exploded, and the other men with him fell to the floor, killed by gunshots in quick succession. Two figures emerged from the gloom of the warehouse, the taller of them standing over Croft. Then a voice said, "Don't fucking call him Raymond."

CHAPTER 9

JACOB HAWK CUT THE TIES THAT WERE SECURING ME FROM behind. As he did so, he said, "This is becoming a habit of late, Mucker."

I stood up on wobbly legs. Marcus Gray, the other man with Hawk, caught me before I fell. "I'm thinking if you want to get up close and personal like this, old mate, you might want to put some clothes on."

"Very fucking funny," I growled. "Give me your sidearm."

Gray shrugged wide shoulders and the Talon operator passed me his P229. Then I took it and shot Croft ten times. With the echoes still ringing in the warehouse, Hawk said, "Fuck, man, you making sure?"

"Bastard took out my tooth."

"Ouch, bet that hurt."

"Well, it wasn't fucking pleasant."

I passed the handgun back to Marcus and began to dress. Jacob Hawk and Marcus Gray worked for Talon. Talon was a team of operatives who led the fight against human trafficking first and foremost but were open to doing other things as well.

Hawk, in his thirties, was former SAS. Gray, late twenties. They were the grunt for the team. Not that the others couldn't handle themselves. They are all experienced operators. "What are you doing here, Jake?"

"Just happened to be in the area. Slick had lost you and wanted to know if the boss could help. Looks like we arrived in the nick of time."

The boss he was talking about was Anja Meyer. She was former German Intelligence and quite a woman. "Not soon enough," I grunted.

"You're still alive."

I rubbed my jaw. "Don't I fucking know it?"

As soon as I was dressed, Hawk said, "Follow us, old son, we'll take you somewhere to get cleaned up."

Outside the warehouse, the sun was going down. I glanced perfunctorily at the sky. I was too pissed to care.

———

"That should see you through," Ilse Geller said as she disposed of the empty penicillin syringe. "Keep any infection at bay. You can pull your pants up now."

Also a German, her touch was soft, her voice calming. I could see why Hawk liked her. But flick her switch, and she was a woman you didn't want to cross. "Thanks."

Slania Albring forced a beer into my hand. "Here, it'll kill the pain."

Former Belgian Special Forces Group, she'd had

three years there and then intelligence. Her long dark hair framed a narrow face. A good portion of her slim but rock-hard body was covered with tattoos.

I said, "I don't think they've made enough of it. Although, it'll possibly keep the pain away long enough for what I have to do next."

"And what would that be?" Anja Meyer asked as she entered the living room, where we were all gathered. She'd just come from the shower and her blonde hair was still wet.

"I'm going after that bitch," I growled.

"Not tonight, you're not. You need rest, Raymond."

I stared at her. If the Raymond was there to bait me, it didn't show. I think that was just the way she was. Very formal.

"I don't have time to rest. She is having a meeting with someone tonight. Once she works out her plan has gone to shit, she could disappear, and we won't know where."

Anja stared at me for several pensive seconds.

"I'm going whether you like it or not."

With a nod, Anja replied, "You are a stubborn man, Raymond. All right. Slania, see if you can find her. Until then, Raymond, you rest."

———

After just one hour, they had located Mary. She was dining at a restaurant in the city. We rolled out straight away. Anja, Ilse, and Slania overseeing our mission on the ground.

Mary was entertaining a Saudi prince who was looking to buy a shipment of the latest assault rifles coming out of the German armed forces. Additionally, he wanted shoulder-launched missiles and some armored SUVs.

With business and dinner completed, her SUV was brought around. She climbed in as normal without acknowledging her driver. Until she saw me sitting on the back seat beside her. "Hello, Mary."

Mary looked down at the Glock I was holding on her. She gave me a weak smile. "So, this is how it's going to be."

Gray pulled away, joining the long line of traffic. Hawk was beside him in the passenger seat.

I said, "You have two choices. You tell me what I want to know, and you get to go home to your kid. You don't, and you won't even leave this SUV. I'm sick of fucking around."

She could tell I was serious. "Okay, what do you want to know?"

"Where is Max?"

"He's headed to England. He might even be there already."

"What does he want with the miniguns?" I asked.

"He is doing a job for someone."

"Who?"

Mary shook her head. "I don't know. We don't ask. We try to keep our clients' names out of it."

"You must have some idea," I said as the SUV sped along the street beneath the orange streetlamps. "Was it the Russians?"

"I—I don't know. Maybe."

"What Russians? Did you get anything?"

"No, nothing."

"Where about in England is he?"

"I don't know. That's all I can tell you."

I stared into her eyes. "Okay, pull us over."

Hawk did just that. I cast one last glance at Mary and said, "Goodbye."

After that, all hell broke loose.

"We're taking fire! We're taking heavy fire. The package is down, and we're pinned down."

"Roger, Bravo One, we're working on the problem," came the reply.

The *problem* started when we opened the doors to the SUV. Two vehicles pulled up in a pincer movement, blocking our vehicle from going anywhere. I don't know how many shooters there were, but they began piling out of the SUVs. Then they opened fire, and someone threw a grenade, and the world turned upside-down.

I was knocked silly, and I think I blacked out for a short period. When I came back around, I could hear Hawk calling it in and Anja's response. I was lying close to Mary's SUV and could see inside. Mary was slumped sideways, her eyes open, part of her skull blown away where a bullet had smashed through it. It looked like the kid was going to be without a mother after all. Shit.

I grabbed my Glock and crawled toward the rear of the SUV. "Someone fucking talk to me."

"About time you joined the land of the living," Hawk said.

I heard Gray say, "We've got multiple shooters bent on ruining our night. We've put a couple down, but there're still enough to go around."

"Roger that." I peered under the rear bumper and saw a shooter partially exposed. I loosed a shot and he fell onto his side. I fired twice more and both bullets found a new home. "Scratch another one."

My actions drew an inordinate amount of return fire, causing me to scuttle back. Bullets kicked up off the pavement, just missing me. I could hear voices calling out. They were Russian. It was unmistakable.

"We've got Ivans in the house," I called out.

"No shit," Hawk called back. "They're mercs."

Mercs? "They have to be Rebrov's men."

"You just love getting in the shit, don't you?"

It was then that things got worse.

"Chaps, you have an SUV coming at you from the east," Ilse warned us.

"Great," I heard Hawk mutter over the comms.

"Could be worse," I said. "It could be a heli—"

"Heads up, we now have a helicopter inbound," Anja said. "I advise you to bug out."

Gray turned and looked at me. "You just had to fucking say it."

"Ah, yes, but I didn't, did I?"

"You thought it. Same thing."

The SUV from the east pulled up, a shooter with an LMG standing out of the sunroof. The light machine gun opened fire and rounds peppered everything like a rainstorm. The worst part about our situation was that we were under a streetlamp. And while we could see them in the light, they could also see every move that we made.

I glanced around, searching for an escape, my eyes

noticed a door into a store almost opposite. "Fuck it. Follow me."

I was up and running, the other two following me just as the helicopter appeared and fired a rocket from one of its pods. It streaked out of the night and buried itself into the SUV with the body of Mary still inside. The explosion was large and loud and helped force us through the doorway that I'd opened when I'd hit it with my shoulder.

The force made me skid across the floor inside, the blow jarring through my body.

I stopped and lay there. "Bloody hell."

"You can say that again," Hawk said.

"Hey, guys," Gray said, his voice was strange. Had a trembling edge to it. "I might need some help."

The shooters on the street had stopped firing for the moment and I crawled across to Gray. Hawk beat me to his friend and said, "Ah, shit, what the fuck did you want to do that for?"

"Don't blame me, I didn't blow the bastard up."

I winced. Gray had a long piece of metal piercing his side. It had gone through flesh and cut its way out the back like a giant skewer. "Jake, keep an eye on the door."

"What are you going to do, Knocker?"

"Can't move him around with that in there, can we. It needs to come out. Now get over to the door."

"I hope you know what you're doing."

Staring at Gray, I said, "This is going to hurt."

"Like that tooth, huh?"

"Shit, not that fucking bad."

He chuckled, and as soon as he did that, I pulled. The metal made a wet sucking sound as it came free.

Gray cried out in pain. "You bastard."

"Be nice," I replied. I looked around. It was a clothing store. I grabbed a shirt off the rack and pressed it against the wound. "Hold that there."

"What about the other one," Gray said through gritted teeth. "It bleeds too."

I grabbed another shirt and stuffed it around the back, using the sleeves to fasten it in place. "That'll do until we get you some medical attention."

"They're coming, Knocker."

I helped Gray to his feet. "Can you walk?"

"I'll manage."

"Right, find us a back way out."

He lurched away while I joined Hawk at the front entrance. The shooters were standing out on the street, cradling their weapons, which appeared to be AK-12s.

"They going to shoot?" Hawk asked.

"No."

"You sure?"

"Maybe." Their weapons came around. "Okay, they're going to shoot."

We turned and ran as a storm of bullets blew apart the front of the store. I felt one round clip my shoulder. The pain, instant, burning. "Bastard."

"Are you okay?" Hawk asked.

"I've been shot, tortured, and had a tooth pulled out. I'm just fine, Jake."

Hawk and I found Gray in the back with the rear door already open. "What took you so long?"

Hawk said, "In case you can't hear, they were bloody shooting at us."

"Is that what that is?" He started to lurch out the door then stopped. "You'd better give me a hand."

"Yeah. Alpha, how far out is that backup?"

"A couple of minutes, Bravo. Just keep moving, we'll track you."

"Roger that."

Starting down the alley at the back, I brought up the rear, giving Hawk and Gray cover. A figure appeared in the doorway where we had just been. I fired three times and he disappeared.

Another shooter appeared and I fired again before turning and running after my friends. More gunfire sounded and I could hear the rounds cracking close as they hammered by. I turned and fired wildly, the aim to put them off their game, not to kill. However, if that happened, then all the better.

I caught up with Hawk and Gray as they passed under a streetlamp. I muttered a curse and raised the Glock in my hand, extinguishing it with a single shot. The area around us went dark. "Keep going, I'll catch you up."

Slipping back into the darkness, I waited for our pursuers. They were careless, the scent of blood in their nostrils overriding all common sense that they should otherwise have had. As the three men reached me, I stepped out and opened fire. Six shots, three kills.

BANG-BANG!

BANG-BANG!

BANG-BANG!

Job done.

I looked back along the alley but saw no one else. It looked like we were good. Behind me, at the mouth of the alleyway, I heard the screech of tires. When I turned, I saw a van, its door open, and Hawk was helping Gray into the back. Help had arrived.

———

"How is Marcus?" I asked Hawk.

"Just about patched up," Hawk told me. "Ilse will take care of him."

"I'm sorry I dragged you into this."

"Don't worry about it. You needed help, and we obliged."

"Yeah, but I'm still sorry."

"Not half as much as they will be," Anja said as she entered the room. She passed me a picture. "This came from Mr. Swift."

It was a picture of a man wearing a long coat and a hat. "Is that Zhirkov?"

"Yes. He slipped up. This was taken a couple of hours ago outside a restaurant in the city. He left by car for an airfield on the outskirts. According to Mr. Swift, he is still there."

I picked up a glass of scotch from beside me and downed it. Then I fixed my gaze on Anja and said, "The one thing I've learned about these bastards is that they don't slip up. If we can see him, it is because he wants us to."

"Then what do you propose we do?" Anja asked.

"I'll go alone."

"I can't in all good conscience let you do that," she replied.

"It's okay. I'm used to it. Plus, it'll still be dark."

"At least let Slania run overwatch for you."

"Sure."

"Good."

"There is one other thing, if I get into trouble, don't come for me. They'll expect that and you'll be walking into an ambush."

"And if you die?"

"Come to my funeral."

I think we'll take another break here," German said. "Be back in thirty minutes."

Leaving the room, we all headed to our respective bath-rooms for much-needed visits, then went once more to the cafeteria, ordered, and sat down. Holly and Knocker sat opposite. My cell rang. I answered.

"Yes?"

"We have a name, Reaper." It was Hunt.

"For who?"

"Hecate. Lash gave us a name."

My pulse quickened. "Who is it?"

He told me. I hung up and looked at Holly and Knocker. "We have a name."

"Who?"

I told them.

We were almost done.

CHAPTER 10

I STOOD ON THE OTHER SIDE OF THE FENCE, LOOKING IN. Everything looked quiet except that the lights were on. Whoever was there was expecting me. Anja had supplied me with all that I needed. A suppressed G36K, ammo, body armor, extra ammo, and over-watch. I was set to go.

Kneeling beside the fence, I cut a hole in the wire big enough for me to gain access. I pocketed the small pair of cutters and said into my comms, "Bravo One, ready."

"Bravo, this is Alpha. Your target is in the building to the left of the hangars. I count five inside. There looks to be four bodyguards and the target."

"Roger that."

Slipping through the ragged hole, I went to work. Slania may have given me a definitive number of X-rays inside the target building, but on the airfield itself, it was a case of deal with the threats as they appeared. Which was going to be constant.

"Target left," Slania said in my ear.

I'd gone no further than a few meters and turned to face the first threat, picked it, and fired two rounds. The target dropped.

"Right."

Turn, fire.

"Threats down."

I kept pressing forward.

"One, target left."

The G36 came around anew, and I fired. The downed man was carrying an AK. Unsuppressed. When he impacted the ground, he squeezed the trigger, and a long burst of gunfire filled the night. "Shit. I guess they know I'm here."

From that moment on, calling targets was secondary as I fought hard to stay alive. Anything that moved was a threat.

Anything that was a threat died.

Ahead of me, two shooters appeared. The G36 belched more rounds and they died. I almost did too. From my right, another assailant appeared. He opened fire, and bullets cut through the air close to my face. I released the assault weapon, the strap arresting its fall. My right hand went immediately to the Glock on my hip, drawing it and bringing it into line in one fluid, practiced movement. I fired three times.

The shooter jerked under each impact before falling to the ground. But I hardly noticed it because I was concentrating on the two killers coming at me that I needed to deal with. The Glock launched more bullets in their direction. The first man dropped his weapon and fell. The second opened fire.

I bent low and returned his volley with one of my own. Crying out in pain, he fell beside his friend.

Walking forward, I could see that the first guy I'd shot wasn't done. So, I shot him again before holstering the Glock and taking up the G36.

"How many more of these bastards are out there, Alpha?" I growled.

"Too many, Bravo. Keep your head on a swivel."

Not even halfway to the target building, I kept sweeping left and right, not bothering about what was behind me because those back there were already dead.

"Bravo One, I have movement—"

"Got it," I replied without waiting for Slania to finish. Headlights flashed onto me as a speeding SUV barreled in my direction. "Bloody hell."

Reaching down, I found a 40mm grenade. I slipped it into the M203 launcher and brought it up. Whoever was in the SUV opened fire. Bullets kicked up around my feet and flew past my head. The grenade launcher beneath the G36 came into line, and I fired.

There was a hollow thunk, and moments later, the SUV exploded in an orange fireball. "Oops."

I opened the loading gate and dropped out the spent grenade. While I was at it, I did a tactical reload and placed a fresh magazine into the G36. "Talk to me, Alpha."

"That looks to be the only vehicle, Bravo. Well done. Now shoot the X-rays coming up on your left."

I suddenly felt like a speed shooter on the range. All for show and not much more. Just as soon as I knocked one target down, another took their place. My trigger finger was working like an epileptic having a seizure. Two for you, two for you, etc., etc.

Soon, there were six down, and my path was clear...for the moment.

"Keep moving, Bravo."

Pressing forward toward the target building, I'd covered ten more meters when I was shot in the chest. Grunting as pain ripped through my body, my legs went, and I buckled at the knees, slowly sinking until I was shot again. "Motherfucker."

"Are you all right, Bravo?" Slania asked hurriedly. "Talk to me."

I rolled onto my side. "I've been shot...twice."

"Shit. Is your body armor compromised?"

"No, but it fucking hurts."

"You've got two shooters closing on you, Bravo. You need to move."

I ignored her. I just wanted to stay here until the pain subsided. Besides, it hurt too much to move.

"Bravo, get up."

"In a moment," I muttered. "Just give me a second."

Listening to the footsteps growing closer, I counted them. There were two killers, as Slania had said. As they drew nearer, I could hear their hushed voices. My greatest hope was that they wouldn't shoot me again.

Figuring that they were close enough, I rolled and fired, killing them both. "Motherfuckers," I growled through gritted teeth.

Climbing to my feet, I kept walking.

"Bravo, left!"

Like an encore, I turned and fired, feeling like the character John Wick. For the next minute or so, the ballet of death continued until I reached the target building. With my back against the metal siding, I dropped the magazines from both G36 and Glock, replacing them with fresh ones. "I'm thinking that I should have brought more ammo," I said over the comms.

The door was unlocked, so I slipped inside and went back to work. The first to die was a man wearing a suit. The second was diagonally across from where I stood. Third and fourth followed their friends in quick succession. That left number five. He was sitting on a chair in the middle of the room.

Frowning, I started to circle around, keeping my gun trained on him. My first question was, how come this man was tied in place? Then I found out why. He'd been shot in the side of the head.

Realizing who it was, I growled, "You have got to be fucking kidding me."

"Say again, Bravo One," Slania said.

"Target secure. Package is down."

———

"What happened?" Anja asked me on my return.

"It wasn't the general."

"Who was it?"

"Stanislav Rebrov," I replied.

Anja frowned. "Why would they kill one of their own?"

"Too many mistakes. These people don't tolerate failure."

"So, what now?" Anja inquired.

"I have to get back to the UK. The election isn't far away and Pridham and Stiles are up to something. Whatever it is, I need to be there to stop it."

"I wish you luck."

I nodded slowly. "Tell me, in your travels, have you ever heard the name Dolos or Hecate?"

"Can't say that I have."

"Fair enough. Where are your lot headed to now?"

Anja said. "Rio, trafficking ring that trades primarily in blonde American women. They need a hard shutdown. However, I can see you home."

I shook my head. "I have one more stop before crossing the Channel. An old friend who specializes in underground shipments. If Stiles wants to get his equipment into England, he'll more than likely need to use him."

"Well, good luck, Raymond."

"Thanks for your help."

I was in Le Havre by midafternoon. Still feeling weary even after sleeping on the flight, I just needed to push through and get on with it. Which was what I was doing. Time was short, and the circumstances called for extreme measures. Since leaving Antwerp, another death had taken place. To most people, a body found on a London street wasn't really news, but to the people in intelligence circles, the death of Kevin Lidell was like an earthquake running through its foundations.

Lidell was MI6's head of London Special Intelligence. He had a network set up through the city that acted like the jungle telegraph. If someone sneezed in Bromley, their nose was wiped in Harrow. It was that good.

With the snake's head removed, as they say, its body will die. That's what his death was designed to do. Which also indicated that he had been onto something or had gotten too close. Holly was looking into it.

Meanwhile, I was in Forêt de Montgeon in Le Havre with an old friend, acquiring the information that I needed.

"Keep talking, Gilly," I encouraged him, pressing the barrel of my Glock harder against his head.

"I told you all I know," Gilly replied. "Honest, Knocker."

Gilly was a former regiment man before getting out and skipping across the Channel. Now he was head of one of the bigger smuggling operations coming out of France. "Bullshit, Gilly, you know more than that."

He glanced at the two dead bodyguards lying beside him. "Shit, man, I thought we were friends."

"We are, but some things trump even friendship. Like some asshole bringing automatic miniguns into my country to do bad things."

"Knocker—"

I shot him in the shoulder. It was quick. The gun moved and I placed the barrel against him and pulled the trigger.

Gilly cried out in pain and fell to the side. He squirmed a bit and looked up at me. "Son of a bitch."

"I'd have called me worse, but that will do," I told him. I changed my aim point with the Glock.

"Okay, okay, I shipped something for him yesterday."

"Where to?" I asked him.

"Into Portsmouth. He traveled with it."

"Where to from there?" I asked.

"I don't know. Honest."

"I'm sorry I had to do this, Gilly," I said to him.

He shrugged. "It'll all come out in the wash, mate."

I knew what he meant and shot him in the head.

"You murdered your friend?" Holland snapped at me.

"If I had left him alive, he would have come after me. He would have done the same thing."

"Just like that?"

"Yes. Until you have walked on the dark side, do not judge."

"That is still murder."

"When it comes down to King and Country, we do what we have to do."

"Was that it?" German asked.

Knocker shook his head. "No, the Russians were still coming after me hard. They made another attempt before I left Le Havre."

"The ferry?"

"Yeah, the ferry."

Boarding the ferry just before dusk, I checked into my cabin and then went on deck to enjoy the view. People were still coming aboard. After all, we were at least a couple of hours out from embarkation time.

Returning inside, I found a secluded table in the café. "Coffee, sir?"

I nodded. "Please."

"White? Sugar?"

"Yes, thank you."

When she returned five minutes later, the coffee was placed before me, the froth on top in the shape of a Christmas tree. As she pulled her arm back from the table, I caught sight of a tattoo. A small star, colored into a solid mass. Normally, I wouldn't have thought much of it, but she also had one behind her ear.

Now they were sending assassins after me. I was beginning to think I should have gone to Cuba with Reaper.

While I drank my coffee, I scanned the café. Unconcerned about being poisoned by it, I knew they would want to make this as public as possible to send a message to MI6. That in itself gave me an advantage.

Now it was a matter of waiting.

By the time my coffee was finished, I had picked out five additional possibilities in the café itself. They obviously meant business. I checked my watch. It wouldn't be long now.

When the fire alarm went off and people started to evacuate the ship, I knew this was it. Remaining in my seat, I waited, my hand gripping the Glock beneath the edge of the tablecloth.

Soon, only eight of us lingered. I assumed, however, that there would be more. The waitress returned to my table and spoke to me, "Hello, Mr. Jensen. General Zhirkov offers his deepest condolences on your imminent death."

"Tell the general to suck my dick...no, on the other hand, I'll do it myself."

Then I fired up through the table and watched as the cold smile disappeared from the bitch's face before she could kill me with the double-edged, hooked knife in her right hand.

She staggered back and fell to her knees. I saw the wound, it wouldn't kill her, but she would be out of action.

After the first shot, things escalated. I threw myself

from the seat I was on and landed behind a table. I have found, in my many travels, that a lot of cafés are small, catering to couples on vacation or couples local to the vicinity. On the ferry, this one was quite large, the only food and beverage provider on the trip across the Channel.

Crawling along the floor to escape the fusillade coming at me from the other shooters, I had only a moment to react when a large figure loomed up in front of me. I rolled and fired twice. The first round hit him in the chest, the second tore an ugly wound through his throat. A ghastly spray of blood painted a table behind him before he fell.

Continuing my plight to escape, I came up onto a knee. Selecting a shooter who was firing at me, I fired once. My bullet was the last thing through his mind.

Before his body hit the floor, I was up and moving. More gunfire came my way and table decorations began a macabre dance. Saltshakers shattered and flew away. More rounds knocked chairs over and I was forced to leap over one falling in front of me.

Firing as I ran, a picture on the wall behind one of my targets fell after being hit. I fired again, and another assailant cried out. He reeled away, taking cover behind a half wall.

The whole time that the fire-fight was happening, the fire alarm continued to peal out over the public address system.

Ducking down behind another table, I waited for a sudden burst of fire before returning it. I blew through the rest of the Glock magazine before reloading. Slapping the fresh magazine home, I took off running once more, firing as I went.

Suddenly, I was out of the open plan café and into the main thoroughfare. A shooter abruptly appeared in front of me, and I crashed into him. As I made contact, he hooked my arm and hip-tossed me away from him.

My momentum was all he needed for it to be successful. I flipped off to the side and crashed through the gift store floor-to-ceiling window. Glass rained down upon me like a cascading waterfall.

Letting out a loud grunt, I rolled aside just as the killer took a shot. The bullet hammered into the floor where I had been lying.

Bringing up my Glock, I fired three times. The shooter staggered back and went down hard. Coming to my feet, I put one into his head to finish him off, then kept running.

A woman stepped out in front of me some ten meters ahead. I stopped, hesitated, and she fired quickly, the bullet flying wide. My Glock roared and her leg kicked out from beneath her, sending her crashing to the floor. A cry of pain and rage escaped her lips and she tried to get up to continue the fight. I hit her in the side of the head with my weapon, knocking her out. "Consider this your lucky fucking day, love."

The plan was to get off the ferry without getting killed. So far, I'd been lucky in one aspect, but I was far from out of the woods. Especially when they upped the ante by throwing a grenade.

It bounced along the floor behind me, the sound making me turn and stare wide-eyed at it. I muttered a curse and threw myself behind a pillar. The blast rocked the ship and tore through everything the splinters touched. I was lucky that one of those things wasn't me.

Not that I got off unscathed. The blast wave threw me across the floor into a fake potted plant. Pain ripped through my back as I crunched into it. "Jesus Christ."

Rolling to one side, I climbed to my feet.

More rounds came in my direction as another shooter appeared. He opened fire and missed. Behind me, a fire extinguisher literally exploded off the bulkhead. I ducked and shot at the new shooter. He staggered back but didn't fall.

Squeezing the trigger to have another go at him, I found that the magazine was empty. Muttering a curse, I reloaded as fast as I could. Meanwhile, the wounded shooter began to bring his own gun up. There was no movie-like slow-motion scene in that moment. Just as he was about to shoot, my Glock snapped into line, and I put a bullet into his head. The floor was splashed with a gory mess of blood and brains.

Moments later, I was flying sideways, the gun lost from my grip, a killer landing blows on me even though we were falling.

Air rushed from my lungs as I hit hard, the killer on top of me. I could hear him snarling in my ear like a vicious dog trying to rip out my throat. In desperation, my elbow came around and caught his jaw. He grunted but remained fixed in position. Repeating the movement twice more, I was finally able to dislodge him.

Rolling away, I came to my feet again. The killer pulled his gun. Mine was out of reach. I dived.

He fired.

I rolled.

He missed.

A stainless-steel rope barrier stanchion arrested my momentum, knocking it over. In desperation, I reached out for it and stabbed it at the shooter. By some miracle, the metal plate base acted like a shield and the bullet screamed off it.

Still holding it high, I came to my feet and pressed forward. The killer kept firing and hitting the plate. Finally, I was close enough to drive it forward into his face.

The shooter let out a cry of alarm and reeled away. He tripped over some debris and fell. It gave me the opportunity I so desperately needed. The bollard came savagely down, and the edge of the plate smashed into his skull, cleaving it open.

Throwing my makeshift weapon away, I looked around for the Glock. It still lay where it had landed, beside a lounge chair, one of many strategically placed around the ship for passengers' comfort.

I bent to retrieve it, then straightened up and looked around. The grenade had done significant damage to the ship's interior, and there were bodies of assassins lying on the floor. A shout from further along the open area drew my attention, and I saw three more killers heading in my direction, their guns raised.

"Bloody hell, where are these bastards coming from?"

They opened fire, and I ran, bursting through a doorway into a stairwell. I was about to head down when a shout from below signaled more assailants. So, I went up. Taking the stairs two at a time, I made it to the next deck. This one held a kids' playroom, a bar, and an open big screen area where passengers could watch the idiot box or face the other way and watch the waters of the Channel slip past.

Heading straight for the children's play area, I took shelter behind a fiberglass tube slide and jungle gym. Crouching down, I waited for the assassins to appear. When they showed their faces, we started dancing again: a swirling waltz of deadly lead.

CHAPTER 11

Upon checking my ammunition, I found only three magazines remained, plus whatever was left in the Glock. The first shooter appeared but I held my fire. No use giving advance warning to the others of my intentions. The killer started sweeping left and right, looking for me. The second killer appeared and went left, doing the same. When the third one showed up, he broke off too. Time to move.

With two in the chest and one in the head, the first killer went down. The second took a round just as he went to fire at me. The bullet from my Glock knocked off his aim, which enabled me to put two more into him. The third killer, however, took advantage of the warning and was firing at me before I could get him in my sights.

A bullet whined off a slide and smacked into the wall behind me. I threw myself down on the rubber-matted floor and was grateful for it. Rolling, I managed to get behind a climbing structure as more bullets searched for me.

Once more, I found myself running. A round clipped my clothing as I zig-zagged, trying to throw the shooter's aim off as an additional shooter joined the fray. Working out that I probably had a better chance of running into a bullet that way, I thought, screw it.

At last, a two-way door appeared in front of me, and I hit it with my shoulder, bursting through to the other side.

When I managed to pull myself up, I found myself in a kitchen. Looking left and right, I noticed that I was backed into a corner. I reloaded my Glock again and picked up a meat cleaver. This wasn't going to be good.

The first shooter burst through the door, his weapon up and ready to fire. Before he could do anything, I threw the cleaver at him. The heavy chopper spun through the air, its gleaming surface catching the light. It was brought to an abrupt halt, buried deep in the forehead of the assassin.

A second shooter came through as the body of his friend fell, and I shot him three times. The bodies were piling up, literally, as the doors swung shut again. After this I changed position, selecting a large-bladed knife from the counter. Pressing my back against the wall near the opening, I waited for the third shooter to enter. He was more cautious than the others had been.

Edging through the opening carefully, his arm extended, weapon in front, I waited for him to get almost through when I brought the knife up savagely and buried it deep into the flesh beneath his chin, the point driving up into his brain.

He stiffened and spasmed before falling forward

onto his face with a sickening sound. Once he was down, I stepped back through the doorway and opened fire again.

A Russian standing just beyond the opening fell, and I shot the one behind him. A third was already firing at me, and I felt the burn of a bullet as it passed through my clothing, scoring a red furrow along my ribs. Through gritted teeth, I cursed him and then shot him in the head.

Not sure exactly of my position on the ship, what I did know was that I needed to get off it. God alone knew how many of them were left. This was the most determined I'd seen them in a good while. Obviously, we were making them nervous.

Suddenly, a rolling, rattling sound caught my attention. I turned to see a grenade rolling across the floor.

"Bloody hell!"

I dived for cover, and moments later, the deadly explosive detonated. Slivers of death scythed above me while the concussive blast shoved me aside like I was an insignificant bug. It still knocked the air from my lungs.

Gasping for breath, I crawled along the floor for another doorway. As I reached it, I stood and looked back. The area was full of smoke and debris. A fire had ignited and was beginning to take hold.

Out of the haze, a shooter appeared, firing wildly at me. I thrust myself backward and crashed into another large floor-to-ceiling window. It shattered and I disappeared within.

A shipboard gift store. I scooted along the floor and

around behind a shelf filled with souvenirs and other items for sale.

Another shooter appeared. This time, a woman who joined her compatriot. The pair opened fire simultaneously at the shelves, and I was forced to drop as low as I could while bullets hammered through the shelves, showering items all around me. My arms covered my head as a can fell on them. I then crawled along the aisle until I reached the end.

From there, I was able to lean around the shelf and fire through the opening where the window had once been. I saw the male assassin jerk as a round found him. He staggered, and my next bullet punched into his head.

Attired comfortably in jeans and a black jacket, the female assassin pointed her handgun at me. I withdrew before she could fire, and I listened as bullets crashed all around me. Next came her shrill cry of frustration as she burned through her magazine until it was empty.

Seizing the opportunity presented to me, I came to my feet and fired. The bullet emitted from the barrel took the woman in the leg.

Reverberating throughout the ship, her agonizing shriek was almost deafening as she collapsed in a heap. Despite her travails, she managed to retain the grip on her gun, bringing it up to take me out.

"Don't," I snapped. I take no pleasure in shooting women, but when the choice came to protecting my own life—

I fired. This time, it was low and left, so that, with luck, it would miss anything vital. No sooner had I fired than I hurried forward and kicked the gun from her hand, keeping her covered with mine. Giving me a hate-filled glare but screwing her eyes up against the pain. Her rage was simmering just below the surface. I grabbed her hand and forced it to the wound in her side. "Keep pressure on this. You'll be fine."

"Fuck you, asshole," she replied, her accent thick.

Suddenly, her concealed radio came to life. There were two more teams on the ship closing on the sound of battle.

Time to go.

Moving briskly toward the stern of the ship, I made it as far as the cabin area. Halfway along a narrow passageway, I was confronted by a figure. They fired wildly at me, the bullet missing me completely but scoring the wall. I dropped low and returned fire, my bullet striking home. The shooter buckled and I ran forward, my foot lashing out, boot connecting with his head in a sickening crunch.

Another assassin stepped into the corridor, and I launched myself at him. My Glock rose and fell, the butt connecting savagely between his eyes. The killer dropped like a stone at my feet, his forehead split, emitting a steady flow of blood from the wound.

Stepping over him, I peered around the corner at a stairwell that would take me to a lower deck and closer to disembarkation.

I took them two at a time, emerging on the deck below where I almost shot one of the staff. My gun was pointed straight at his face.

"Don't shoot!"

"Bloody hell, what are you still doing here?" I growled.

"Making sure everyone got off. What are you doing here?"

"Doing my best to bloody stay alive. Come on, let's—"

A shot cracked loudly, and a bullet smashed into his back. He lurched forward and fell onto his face. Totally incensed, I shot the perpetrator many times. I can't be sure of the count because the curtain of rage came down and took over.

That left me with just one magazine, not ideal. I reloaded and double-checked the downed steward. As I suspected, he was dead. The radio carried by the dead assassin crackled to life. The first words were demanding, then became anxious. I picked up the radio and said in Russian, "Your man is dead, asshole."

"Who is this?"

"Your worst fucking nightmare. See you on deck."

With determined resolve, instead of heading down to leave the ship, I went up. Before I did, however, I requisitioned the dead assassin's P-96. Compact and easy to hide, I stuffed it into my pants and began climbing the stairs.

I found the deck mostly clear. It was open in places but had clutter as well. Plenty of places to take cover. Not planning to hide, I was done with running.

Walking steadily toward me were three men, all armed. I stood resolute, two guns in my hands like a shootout in an old western movie. "Only three of you left? You should quit now before you join your friends."

"Your run of luck stops here," the man in the center said with finality.

"Call it."

My demise could have resulted so many times, but not this one. Bullets flew, guns fired, men died, and not one of them was me. I walked across the deck to where the Russians lay. All were dead, and I could still hear the fire alarm sounding over the public address system.

I needed another way to get home.

It was midnight by the time I finally arrived in London. Holly and Slick collected my sorry ass from the airport. As soon as she saw me, she said, "You look like shit, Ray."

"Everywhere I go, people are trying to kill me. They aren't letting up. Just a little rest would do me the world of good."

Holly said, "You can rest when you are dead. Tell me a story."

"Max Stiles came into Portsmouth with two mini-guns. I have no idea what he's up to, but you can bet it has something to do with the election. Speaking of which—"

"Since the bombings, Pridham has surged in the polls. It looks like it'll be close. All he needs is something to tip him over the edge."

"Which means we can expect that something to happen soon."

"Yes. Do you know anything else?"

"Not a lot. Max Stiles is the best lead," I replied. "Anything on Hecate?"

"No."

As we drove through the London night, a heavy shower began to fall from the leaden sky. The roads became slick and the journey miserable. "Where are we headed, Holly?"

"Pridham is holding a rally tomorrow, and we're going to be there. Until then, I need to put you somewhere safe so you can sleep."

"Where might that be?"

"My place."

———

Ten minutes later, we pulled up on a narrow street outside a Brownstone terrace. Climbing from the vehicle, I followed my team mates inside. Slick immediately set to work on his computer keyboard. "That goes for you too, Slick," Holly told him. "In my spare room."

"Yes, boss."

Once he was gone, Holly turned to me and said, "Clothes off."

With a sigh, I said, "I don't think I could manage."

"Don't be a dick," she said abruptly. "Take them off, I want to check you over."

"Yes, ma'am."

While I stripped down to my underwear, Holly went to her bathroom and found her first aid kit. It wasn't your normal family-friendly one. This box would have made a combat medic proud to use it. I wasn't cold because she had central heating. Staring at my body, she shook her head. "You look a little banged up, Ray."

"I'll live."

"There are a lot of bruises and small cuts, but this one here will need stitching." Holly touched my side.

I winced. Then I felt the burn of pain. I recalled the bullet grazing my side.

She held up a fragment of glass in bloody fingers. "This yours?"

"Went through a window. Actually, make that two windows."

Holly opened the kit and set out everything she needed to sew the wound shut. "I'm sorry, I don't have any local."

"I'll be right. Get it done."

After ten minutes of carefully jabbing me with the needle, the wound was closed, had antiseptic slathered on it, and was covered with a dressing. "Don't pop them," Holly warned me.

"I can't promise that."

"No, I don't suppose you can. The dressing is waterproof, so you'll be good to have a shower."

I stood up and swayed, grabbing the side of the table to steady myself. Holly latched onto my arm. "Steady, big boy."

Without thinking, I rested my head on her shoulder. "I'm thinking maybe it has all caught up with me, boss."

"Yeah, maybe I was wrong about that rest. Come on, I'll help you into the shower."

"I can manage," I said, straightening.

"Becoming shy, Ray? It's not like I haven't seen what you've got."

I chuckled. "It's not that."

"Then what?"

"I'm afraid you won't be able to resist once you see

me naked, and I'm too fucked to do anything about it."

"Come on, Casanova."

I don't think I've ever felt so tired before. After all that had happened, I was totally rooted. Once I was washed, I climbed out and dried myself, wrapping the towel around me because Holly had my clothes in the wash.

I walked out into the kitchen, and she gave me a coffee laced with scotch. "That tastes good."

"Drink it and go to bed."

"Sofa?"

"No, my bed."

"I told you," I said with a tired grin.

"I'll try to refrain. Although, I'm not sure how I'll manage it, sleeping beside a naked stud like you."

"Now you're just taking the piss."

"Yes, I am."

Five minutes later, I was in a soft bed wrapped in Egyptian cotton sheets. Sixty seconds later, I was asleep.

———

When I awoke the next morning, I thought maybe I was still in Antwerp with a hot blonde beside me, trying to work out how she got into my bed. Then I realized it was Holly wearing bugger all.

My mind flicked back through the replay of the night before and when I realized nothing had happened, I was more than a little relieved. I swung my legs out over the side of the bed and looked down, suddenly aware that I was totally naked.

"Your clothes are in the dryer," Holly said.

Finding my clothes, I pulled them on. By the time I was dressed, Holly had risen and was busy preparing a hearty breakfast. Slick was already on his computer working, giving a cheery wave in my direction as I entered the kitchen. Holly cooked bacon, eggs, and toast. A plate of food in front of us, we started to eat.

Around a mouthful of bacon, she said, "Pridham has that rally this morning. Once we finish here, we'll head out."

"What is the rally about?"

"Just to drum up support. It's the first of two happening over the next three days before everyone votes."

"Where is the one being held today?" I asked, taking a sip of my coffee.

"London Stadium. The second is at Wembley."

"It won't be today, which gives us a bit more time. But I still want to go there."

Holly stared at me across her plate. "I've seen that look before, Ray. What are you up to?"

"I'm going to shake the prick's tree and see what comes loose."

"Oh boy, that's bad."

"Well, you won't like what I'm about to suggest," I replied.

"I'm loath to ask, but…"

"I kill him."

"Damn, Ray, you can't do that," Holly almost exploded. "He is a British citizen in a high office—"

"He's not a fucking British citizen. He's a Russian mole who is going to take over our country—our country, Holly—from the inside. He and the bastards with him must be stopped."

She stared at me thoughtfully. "Just shake his tree, okay? Don't do anything stupid."

"You know me."

"Yes, I do, that's why I said it."

"Slick, I'm going to need comms and overwatch," I called over to him. "Also, I'm going to need to be able to carry a weapon."

Holly surprised me by saying, "No weapons."

"You ruin all a man's fun."

"Don't I know it."

CHAPTER 12

THE RALLY REMINDED ME OF AN AMERICAN CONVENTION. The atmosphere was electric. Excitement and an undying devotion for the delegate tipped to become the next PM. And Fergus Pridham was taking full advantage of his new-found fame.

Slick's main job was to scan the heaving throng for familiar faces. It didn't take him long to find one. "You are not going to believe this. Or maybe you will because nothing really surprises you. On the other hand—"

"Slick, spit it out."

"I just picked up Oleg Zhirkov," he informed me.

"Where?" I asked, standing on a step and looking around the packed crowd.

"Going into the room where Pridham is."

"Guide me there."

I made my way down the stairs of the section of the stadium and into the bowels of the structure itself. I managed to bypass security by flashing the ID supplied by Holly. Inside the large room where

Pridham had gone, his personal security detail and staff milled around.

Off to one side, I saw Pridham talking to Zhirkov. With others in the room seemingly too busy to notice, I pegged three big, burly-looking brutes as the Russian's detail.

Walking toward them, I was brought to a halt when one stepped in front of me. He gave me a look which told me I was to go no closer.

I said, "If you don't move, mate, I will walk right over you."

He remained unmoving.

I switched to Russian. "In case you didn't understand me, fuck off."

"Great way to make friends, Ray," Holly said.

Both Pridham and Zhirkov stared at me. Pridham asked, "Is there a problem?"

A smile came to my lips, and I did what any normal person would do. I waved. "Hey Fergus, Oleg, how's things?"

Pridham frowned. "Do I know you?"

"You should, but maybe we need to carry on this conversation without anyone else here."

"I don't have time for—"

A hand from Zhirkov rested on Pridham's arm. A look from the Russian was enough for Pridham to say, "Everyone out."

As expected, there were protests, but the politician was more than insistent. "Out, now."

With everyone else gone, it left me, Pridham, and Zhirkov. It was the Russian who spoke first. "You are a persistent man, Mr. Jensen."

I nodded. "Like a dog with a bone. However, we're

not here to talk about me. I'm here to ask Fergus to reconsider his run for office."

"Why would I do that?" Pridham asked.

"Because I don't want a Russian as my PM."

"What are you talking about?"

A knock at the door and a head appeared. "Sir, you're due on stage."

"I'll be there in a moment." He turned his attention back to me. "I have no idea what you are on about?"

"You are a dumb motherfucker," I snarled. "You are a puppet for Lash. Your grandfather was part of the Gods, just like Oleg here. Since we're talking straight, try this. If you don't stop, I'm going to put every one of you pricks in the ground."

I began walking toward the door before I stopped and turned back. "And, Oleg, I'm putting you in the ground no matter what. Get ready, you Russian bastard, I'm fucking coming for you."

Then I left. But not the stadium. I wanted to see what this guy was feeding the masses that they were lapping up.

I found a seat between two guys. One looked like his diet had consisted of hamburgers for most of his life, while the other seemed to have been lucky to eat once a week. They appeared polar opposites but were geared up, ready to support the Russian who was about to lay down shit, and they were going to eat it.

The big guy looked at me and spoke. "This is going to be great, pal. I cannot wait for Fergus to get started. He's going to be so great for this country."

"If you say so."

The man raised his eyebrows. "You don't like him?"

"Let's just say the jury is out."

Suddenly the crowd erupted, and I saw the reason why. Pridham was making his way to the podium to begin his speech. He was flanked by two bodyguards. There was no sign of Zhirkov. I looked around, but there were too many people. He was obviously hiding somewhere in the wings.

Pridham climbed the steps and stood there, taking in the rapturous applause. It took two minutes for the place to quieten down, and then he began a long, droning monologue. However, ten minutes in, his voice changed, and he started to tell the people what they wanted to hear. How he was going to fix the economy, how he was going to get everyone jobs, how he was going to recall troops from overseas to protect their borders from the influx of refugees across the Channel, and how he was going to make amends with all those that Britain had wronged. And they all lapped it up. For a full forty minutes, he rambled on, blaming all of the UK's problems on the party in charge of the country.

The current Prime Minister was no good. His government was no good. His decisions were no good. He had to go. And the only way to do it was to be sent packing by the voters. He said, "A vote for me is a vote for change, and a vote for change will fix everything."

Then he started on the terrorist attacks. They were the fault of the immigrants. And the only way to stop the immigrants was to bring the members of the British Armed Forces back. They belonged on home soil where they could protect everyday citizens from the threats. "Vote for me, and I will recall them for your protection. Together, we can do this, but I need your help. You must vote. Not for the current Prime Minister. Not for any other party. But for me, make Fergus Pridham your Prime Minister!"

The last two words were shouted at the top of his voice. The stadium erupted in shouts and applause. Pridham stood there with arms wide. Every now and again, he would bow.

Unable to take any more, I rose from my chair and moved to leave. The big guy grabbed my arm and said to me, "Are you leaving already?"

"Yes, I've seen enough."

"You should hang around, man. He's still got at least another half hour to go."

I shook my head and kept walking. Even five minutes later, when I was beyond the arena's outer walls, I could still hear the noise from inside. "Where are you, Holly?"

"Coming at you."

The SUV pulled up in front of me and I climbed in. Slamming the door, I looked across at her. "That is one crazy motherfucker."

"What now?" she asked me.

"I don't know."

"Do you think your words had any effect?"

"Oh, yes, they had an effect. The question is, what are they going to do about it? I figure it'll be one of two things. They will ignore it. Or they'll come after me very hard."

It turned out to be the latter.

———

We picked up a tail soon after leaving the rally. It was the standard black SUV, dark windows and the rest of it. Just like in the movies. "Do you see it?"

Holly nodded. "We'll see if they follow us to Whitehall."

They did. But there was another surprise waiting for us when we arrived. An irate Christine Ryan with a message from a man who was once a top FSB official.

Entering the building, we hurried along to the operations room. Slick had met us there and was already working. I said, "Find me a black SUV that doesn't belong."

"Company?" he asked.

"Yes. I'm thinking they are Zhirkov's people."

"Let's see—"

"You two, a word, now."

I turned to see Christine Ryan looking more than a little unhappy. I knew what was coming. I have that effect on some people.

However, it was Holly who spoke first. "Ma'am—"

"Don't say a word, Miss Smith. Not until I talk to our mutual fuck up here."

"Lovely to see you too, ma'am," I replied, pretending to doff a hat at her.

"Don't you fucking dare. What the hell were you thinking? I just got off the phone with Fergus Pridham, who—"

"Fuck him."

"What?"

"You heard me," I snapped back. "I'm sorry, but I bet what he failed to inform you was that when I was there talking to him, he was with Oleg Zhirkov."

Christine Ryan stared at me. "Zhirkov? As in Russian General Oleg Zhirkov?"

"Yes, ma'am. And I must have struck a chord because they had someone following us."

"You threatened to kill him," she replied. "He told me."

"Not technically true. I said I'd put them in the ground. I didn't say I would kill them beforehand."

"Bloody semantics, Raymond."

"Somehow, we have to get them to unravel," I told her.

"Not by walking up to him and threatening him with death," Christine Ryan retorted. "Find another way. At this point in time, he's going to be the next PM, and the intelligence services are at the top of his list to overhaul."

"What do you mean?" Holly asked.

"I have it on good authority that Six and Five are to be dissolved and placed under the auspices and watchful eyes of the Prime Minister's office."

"That's bollocks."

"That's what's going to happen."

A young woman appeared with a piece of paper in her hand. Christine Ryan turned her head and glared at her. "Can't you see we're in the middle of something?"

"Yes, ma'am, but I have a message for Miss Smith. It looks to be important."

"Fine, fine."

The young woman handed the message over and Holly looked at it. Christine Ryan raised her eyebrows. "Well?"

"Someone has reached out claiming they have intelligence."

"About what?"

"I don't know, but he is asking for Ray. Says he wants to meet him within the hour."

"Fine, go. I'm done here anyway. I have a flight to catch. Just stay out of trouble while I'm gone."

"Yes, ma'am."

She walked away and Holly gave me the note. "Do you know him?"

It was my turn to look at it. I nodded. "I do."

"Then you'd better go and see him."

"Yes."

I had.

———

The park was a manicured green beneath a drab gray sky. I wandered through to the meeting place, keeping an eye out for anything suspicious. Watching my six was Slick. "Looks clear so far, Knocker."

"Yeah, so far."

"How do you know this guy, anyway?" he asked me.

"Fyodor was FSB. He was based in Lithuania some years ago when I was there looking for a Russian spy who had gone rogue and was taking out our agents and selling weapons. He was doing the same thing."

"Did you get him?"

"Eventually."

I continued strolling toward the pond and noticed a man feeding the ducks from a park bench. I sat down beside him. "Hello, Fyodor."

"Hello, Raymond."

"Been a while."

"Yes, old friend, it has."

"What do I owe the pleasure?"

"I have something for you. Information."

"About what?" I asked.

"Oleg Zhirkov."

"I already know about him, Fyodor. He's in London."

He shook his head. "No, he left straight after the rally. He's headed to Yorkshire until after the election."

"How do you know all of this?" I asked him.

"I still have many friends, Raymond. We can see what is coming. It is all bad. We have been following your progress in the battle against the Generals with interest."

"Are you in with Boris Pushkin?" I asked him.

He shrugged. "Let's just say we have mutual enemies."

"Why are you telling me about Zhirkov?"

"Because you should get him while he's not expecting it."

"I have something else to do. Max Stiles is up to something, and I need to stop it."

"I will take care of Max Stiles," Fyodor said. "You take care of Zhirkov."

I nodded. "Okay."

Fyodor stood up, shaking the rest of the bread out of the brown paper bag. "Good. I wish you luck, Raymond."

"You too, Fyodor."

Before walking away, he gave me a small folder. "Everything is in there."

———

Five minutes later, I was back in the SUV with Holly and Slick. Holly said, "What are you going to do?"

"Go after Zhirkov."

"Do you trust him to get Max Stiles?"

"I guess I'll have to."

On top of the file that Fyodor gave to me, I saw a photo of a farmhouse. There was an address below it. As I worked my way through the folder, I said, "We're going to need a team."

"Why?" Holly asked.

"Because I plan on bringing him in alive. If we can capture him, we can fly him out."

"Ah, no, not going to happen," Slick said.

I turned to face him. "Why not?"

"There is a big storm moving in. It's going to be over the upper part of the country for a couple of days, starting tonight. If you get him, you won't be flying anywhere."

"Shit. We'll have to drive."

"I'm not sure about this, Ray," Holly said to me.

"Just get me some wheels and a team. I'll worry about the rest."

———

Not your average team. It was made up of dark operators who used names like Wolf, Hound, Jock, Sunshine, Lion, Tag, and Fletch. Sunshine was the crew's only woman but an experienced operator.

Darkness would soon be upon us, and the weather

had deteriorated rapidly, closing in with serious ferocity, sending snow pelting down.

Dressed for the conditions, we were ready to move under the cover of darkness. Provided with maps and photos of the farm, we also had all the intel we'd need to complete the operation. As far as I knew, Zhirkov was on site.

Our team approached the perimeter, taking advantage of the darkness and the snowstorm. I kneeled at the edge of the woods, flanking the farm, when Sunshine stepped up beside me. "The rest of the lads, ready?" I asked her.

"Locked, cocked, and ready to rock," she whispered.

Did I mention she was Australian? She was former army.

"They're all set on the perimeter," she continued. "Just give the word, and we're in."

I said into my comms, "Standby."

Before giving the order to move, I performed another scan of the farm. I could see two sentries doing what they could to stay out of the weather. Other than that, there were lights on inside and nothing else. But there was always something else. The laws of averages proved it.

"Snipers take the sentries."

As I watched on, the snipers fired. Due to the conditions, they were both difficult shots. However, these shooters were good, and both sentries went down.

"Okay, move in."

Every one of us moved as a single entity. We came up from our resting position, weapons raised, and pressed forward. We were almost invisible, our white snowsuits blending against a backdrop of snow. Everything seemed to be going well, until it wasn't.

Suddenly, the night lit up as a flare was tripped. I could hear cursing over my comms, knowing that if I didn't take control, things could quickly escalate out of hand. "Keep pressing forward! Snipers, take all targets."

Gunfire erupted from an upper window. The snap of rounds close could just be heard against the noise of the storm. I opened fire with my G36. Beside me, Sunshine did the same. The rest of the team pressed forward. More shooters appeared on the ground, drawing fire from other members of the assault team.

Beside the farmhouse, trekking through a snow flurry, a shooter materialized. I opened fire and saw him fall into a drift. The firing peaked and then abated as we grew closer to the structure. Over my comms, I heard, "Team Two at the back door. Holding."

"Team Three at the front. Holding."

"This is Team lead. Breach now. Don't wait for us."

"Roger that."

I heard the explosions as the teams went in. Their voices came across the comms net as they cleared rooms until just as we entered, I heard Tag say, "Clear up."

Then another voice said, "Still clearing down—fuck."

Gunfire ripped through the lower floor of the farmhouse. "Follow me, Sunshine."

"On your six, boss."

Traversing a hallway toward the sound of the gunfire, we turned a corner and I saw Hound with his shoulder pressed against a wall. Wolf was backed up behind him. "What do we have?"

"Two shooters dug in like ticks on a ball sack."

I called out in Russian, "Comrade, it is time to forget this foolishness."

A shouted "Fuck you!" was followed by a long burst of gunfire. I grabbed a stun grenade and pulled the pin. Looking across the gap, I gave Hound a nod. His bearded face took on a stern expression and he returned the nod with one of his own. I tossed the stun grenade through the opening and watched the two operators go to work.

Moments later, the Russians within were down, and the room was secure. I entered the space and looked around. "He's not here."

Sunshine nodded. "I sure as shit don't see him."

"This is Bravo One to all callsigns. No sign of Lenin. I say again, no sign of Lenin. Start a sweep of the whole property, outbuildings included. I want to know where the bastard is. Snipers, I want all the vehicles brought in. Out."

Each member of the team spent the next ten minutes searching the farmhouse in search of the elusive Zhirkov. It was during the eleventh minute that Tag called in and said, "I've got something in the cellar, Knocker."

"On our way."

Sunshine and I headed down the stairs and found Tag and Lion standing next to a cupboard. "What have you got?"

"The old hidden door behind the cupboard in the cellar trick, boss."

"Open it."

Pushing the cupboard aside, they paused before breaching. Once again, a stun grenade was deployed first. After they entered, I heard a scuffle followed by the cries of all clear from the two men within.

Sunshine and I entered to find Tag restraining a man. "I believe we have what we want," he said, giving me a broad grin.

Standing the man up and turning him to face me, I found myself staring at a familiar mug. Boris Pushkin. "What the fuck is going on?"

———

"What are you doing here, Boris?" I asked the oligarch.

"You fool, you just killed all of my men," he snarled at me.

"What the bloody hell are you doing here, Boris? Why haven't MI6 got you stashed away somewhere?"

"Because I told them I could take care of myself."

"Do they know you are here?"

"No, no one knew."

"Well, yes, they did. How do you think I got here? Christ."

"Who?" he demanded. "Who told you I was here?"

"Fyodor—"

"That bastard," he growled. "Fuck his mother. He is a traitor to our country."

"Are you saying he knew you were here and used us to get to you?"

"Yes. He is eliminating the competition."

"What competition?" I asked.

"To be the next president of Russia," Pushkin spat.

"Shit, boss, we're stuck in the middle of a Russian civil fucking war," Sunshine stated.

"They seem to miss the main point of the picture, Sunshine," I replied. "Lash is the president, and he's not going anywhere."

Pushkin shook his head. "His government will fail, leaving a vacuum in its place. We are vying for the position of the next president. We are all threats to Lash, which is why we are all in hiding. Biding our time."

"A word, boss," Sunshine said.

I turned to look at her, and she began to lead me to the far corner of the room. "What is it?"

"This is fucking crazy. We're being used as pawns in someone else's fight. That Fyodor prick sent us here to either kill him or to flush Pushkin out so he could do the job himself."

Nodding, I said, "You're right. But it's the knock-on effect I'm worried about."

"What do you mean?"

"I'll explain in a moment. Bravo One to Mother, over."

"This is Mother," Holly said. "Traffic not good, you're breaking up."

"Bollocks." I grabbed my cell and made the call. Holly answered. "Can you hear me better now?"

"Just."

I filled her in on what Pushkin had told me. "Bloody hell. That means—"

"Yeah, no one is looking for Max Stiles."

"What are you going to do, Ray?"

"Nothing is flying in this shit," I said about the

weather. "I'll stick with the plan. Drive back to London."

"Be careful, the storm up that way is really bad."

"We'll be fine. Just find Stiles. Call Cara at Global. Have her deploy a strike team to help out."

"I'll see what I can do. Good luck, Ray. Let me know if you need anything."

"Roger that." I disconnected the call and turned to Sunshine. "Get them ready, Sunshine, it's time to go."

CHAPTER 13

THE SNOW WAS THICK ON THE GROUND AND THE ROAD was almost impassable as our four-vehicle convoy battled its way through the howling blizzard. We were in the lead and our vehicle hit a hole in the narrow road and lurched violently. I looked across at Tag and said, "What the fuck was that?"

He shrugged broad shoulders and said, "Who knows, I can't see shit in this whiteout. We're bloody barmy if you ask me."

"We need to get Pushkin back to London by tomorrow," I reminded him.

"Well, we aren't going to fucking get there."

He was right.

"Yeah, well, you and I know that," I replied.

"One, copy?" It was Sunshine.

I reached for the radio. "What's up?"

"This is bollocks. We need to find a place to pull up. I can't see shit and I'm not even fucking driving."

"You know of somewhere?" I asked.

"There is a village about a mile to the west of us," she replied. "The turn should be just down the road."

"If we can bloody find it," Tag growled.

Suddenly, the SUV swerved and skidded off the road into a ditch. Tag smashed his hand on the steering wheel and cursed. He tried to back it out, but the wheels kept spinning on the slick verge. "That fucked it."

"Everybody hold up," I said over the comms. "We've hit a snag."

Opening the door, I let in a blast of icy air. Pulling my snow coat about me even tighter, I walked around the vehicle and knew immediately we were going nowhere. I returned to the front of the SUV and grabbed the radio. "Sunshine, close up, we're going to need a tow."

"Roger that."

Meanwhile, Sunshine glanced at Lion. "This is fucking crazy."

"You know what we need?" Lion asked with a grin.

"If you say a little sunshine, I'm going to cut your fucking balls off, Lion."

It had been a running joke since the formation of the team. Sunshine was a good operator, even if she was a little on the short side. She got Lion to move the SUV forward to where they could hook the winch up to our vehicle. Once he stopped, Sunshine pulled the hood of her coat up over her blonde hair and climbed out. Lion did the same thing.

I was already using the remote on the front bumper to run out the winch cable.

"Tag screw up again?" Sunshine asked with a grin.

"The only thing Tag screws is you," Lion called out against the howling wind.

Sunshine turned and poked her tongue out at him.

Connecting the winch hook up to the tow point under the rear of the SUV, I said, "Let's see if that works."

The winch motor began to whir, its cable winding in, and almost immediately, Lion's SUV started sliding forward. She shook her head. "Nope."

"All right. Lion, get Hound up here. We'll hitch him up to make a bigger anchor point. Hopefully that will work."

The snow continued to float down in fat flurries all around us, the wind getting stronger and whipping them away before they could hit the ground. I felt its bite even more so now than when I had first climbed out of the SUV.

Hound's SUV came forward to hook up their winch. They spooled out a few meters of cable and then started winching our stuck vehicle back onto the road.

Minutes later, the SUV was ready to go.

"Why would you try such a venture in the first place?" German asked. *"You knew the weather was bad. Why not just sit it out where you were?"*

"Because if Fyodor was going to come after us, that was where it would be. I wasn't about to wait there and find out," Knocker replied.

"Instead, you started south in a brutal storm and had to seek shelter anyway."

"Yes."

"He made the right choice," I said, backing my friend's decision.

"Really?" Holland asked. "I'm not too sure about that."

"How would you know? You weren't there."

I glanced at Newman who remained silent.

"Then convince us, Mr. Jensen," German said, gesturing to the panel. "Convince us."

Meanwhile, Pushkin sat waiting for us to finish stuffing around. Fletch was keeping an eye on him from the front passenger seat. The strength of the wind gusts kept buffeting the SUV. Hound appeared and climbed back in, shaking his head. "This is fucking bullshit."

"It's a crazy motherfucking day to be on the road," Pushkin said to no one in particular.

Fletch turned and glared at him. "How about you shut the fuck up."

"Just saying is all. Besides, if it wasn't for you lot, I would be warm and dry in my farmhouse, and we wouldn't be here."

"What makes you so important, anyway?" Fletch demanded.

Pushkin stared at the operator with the dark goatee beard. "Circumstance, my friend. It all comes down to circumstance."

"I'm not your fucking friend."

I had chosen them to watch over Pushkin because they were good, not friendly.

Pushkin stared out the window through the flurries of snow.

Once all the vehicles were unhooked, Sunshine came over to me. "We should keep going to Glamorgan."

"What is there?" I asked.

"It's an old village. Last time I was there, it was almost deserted. But we will have shelter."

"Fine. You lead."

I climbed back into the SUV and said, "We're headed for Glamorgan."

"Wales?" Tag asked.

"No dipshit, the village. Sunshine suggested that it would be a good place to take shelter."

"Never heard of it."

I grunted. "You're about to see it."

———

We waited for Sunshine to start moving, then fell in behind her. After all, she knew the way. Once again, it was slow going as we drove through the snow-covered, blizzard enshrouded landscape.

Although not physically connected, the convoy acted like train carriages, surging and then going faster before slowing again.

"What's in Glamorgan, anyway?" Tag asked.

"About the same thing that's in your virgin sister, mate. Fuck all."

"People?"

I shrugged. "Not sure."

The road snaked through an S-bend and crossed a stone bridge over a snow-choked stream. As we climbed a small hill on the other side, brake lights came on.

"Sunshine is slowing. We must be coming onto the turn," I pointed out.

"Are you sure?" Tag asked.

"Of course, I'm sure. What else would it be? She slowed down."

Then the vehicle in front stopped and Sunshine's voice came over the comms, "Heads on a swivel."

I frowned, gripped the butt of my P30, and said over the radio, "What the hell is this?"

Tag slowed just short of the intersection and stopped before he could run into the back of Sunshine's SUV.

"I have a man in the middle of the road, waving us down," she replied.

"Who the fuck is out in weather like this?" I growled.

Up front, Lion reached for his handgun and lay it on his lap. The man came up to the passenger window, an expression of relief on his face. The window came down and the warm air inside the SUV was forced out by the cold blast.

The man said, "Boy, am I glad to see you. Our vehicle is stuck fast in the snowdrift."

The accent was American. Sunshine looked to where he was pointing and saw the dull glow of tail-lights sitting in the darkness off the side of the road. "How did you end up in there?" she asked.

"You don't want to know." He stomped his feet, trying to keep warm. "Can you help us out?"

"Who is us?" Lion asked.

"Me and my fiancé, Laura. I'm Glen, by the way. We're from Helena in Montana."

Sunshine nodded. "Let's have a look at your situation."

Glen smiled. "Great."

"One, we have a couple with their vehicle stuck in the snow."

"I'm on my way up," I replied.

Taking a couple deep breaths of warm air, I started to climb from the SUV, speaking to Tag before closing the door. "Remember, keep your head on a swivel."

I walked along the icy road, past Sunshine's still-running SUV, and stopped at the vehicle. It was a Peugeot sedan, and it was stuck fast. I shook my head at Sunshine. "That's going nowhere. They'd better come with us."

"You sure, boss?"

"Can't leave them out here to die."

The man looked uncertain. "Only if you're sure."

"We're just going down that way to Glamorgan," Sunshine explained, pointing to the road running perpendicular to the one we were on. "You might be able to call for some help from there."

"Might?"

"Yeah, Glamorgan is a small village, getting smaller the last time I was there."

"Oh, okay, if you're sure."

"Well, like the boss said, you could always stay here and die."

I turned and started back to the SUV. I climbed in and watched as Glen helped his fiancé out of the Peugeot. They hurried back to our vehicle and climbed in. "Thanks for this, really. This is Laura. I'm Glen."

"Hello." She greeted us with a joyous, bordering on ridiculous, wave.

I was already starting to regret my decision. Glen said, "Who is your friend?"

"Shut up, you're hurting my ears," Tag replied.

"Okay, the talkative type."

Tag engaged the SUV into drive and the convoy started off once more, following Sunshine.

"Who the fuck do you figure they are?" Lion asked. Both held handguns in their laps.

Sunshine shrugged. "Some useless prick who can't drive. Hey, Jensen, have you been giving out driving lessons again?"

"Shut your hole, woman," I said over the radio.

Sunshine grinned at the banter.

We took the turn and continued to fight the blizzard as we drove toward our destination.

———

"All communications are down," Sunshine said to me after we entered the old pub. "This storm has fucked everything up."

I nodded. "I half expected it would. Tag, Hound, go back out and see if you can find anyone."

"Out there, boss?"

"Yes."

They disappeared and I turned to Wolf. "Get a fire going."

"Jock, get out there and find a good overwatch position."

"Knocker—"

"I'm not saying in the snow. Find somewhere sheltered."

"There's no power," Lion informed us.

"Not surprised. Could be the storm or just because no one is here."

"What would you like us to do?" asked Glen.

"Nothing," Sunshine said. "Just stay out of the way."

We set up in the pub and got a fire going. The others returned with the news that the village was deserted. "Not a sign of life anywhere."

"All right, get some rest. Tag, take over from Jock in an hour. I don't want anyone out there in the cold for more than that."

"Got it."

For the next three hours the storm kept on unabated. The wind howled and the snow came down like white sheets. It was what those in weather circles called a one-in-a-hundred-year storm.

Lion was on watch when things changed. It was four in the morning, and the storm still hadn't eased. He came inside and woke Sunshine, who in turn woke me. "Wake up, boss, we might have a problem."

"What is it?" I asked through my sleep-fuddled fog.

"Get up."

I got up and met Sunshine and Lion near the fire, which was still burning fiercely. Lion said, "I think I heard snowmobiles."

"Snowmobiles?" I was skeptical.

"Yes."

I thought for a moment. To dismiss it out of hand was to be careless. I nodded. "All right, get Tag and Wolf. We're going out."

"I'll come with you," Sunshine said.

"No. You watch over our guest. If—"

A sudden commotion from the far end of the bar drew our attention. Glen was struggling with Pushkin.

What I misinterpreted as a misunderstanding became clearer when I saw that Glen had a knife. I didn't have a clear shot, but Sunshine did. She brought up her Glock and fired twice. Glen, or whoever he was, cried out in pain and fell to the old pub's slate floor.

"Where's his woman?" I called out.

Confusion reigned as we all looked around. Then came a couple of gunshots. One was from the woman who fell wounded to the floor, the other from Lion. She was quickly disarmed and restrained.

Having been shot in the shoulder, she was dragged to her feet by Lion. Spitting and kicking, she needed some persuasion to settle her down. That was willingly supplied by Sunshine, who hit her with a clenched fist. "Settle the fuck down, bitch."

The woman we knew as Laura started to swear at her in French. I nodded. "Wasn't expecting that."

She cursed me and spat in my direction. So, Sunshine hit her again. "Shut up."

Moving closer to her, I said in French, "Who are you?"

She just glared at me.

"Are they your friends out there on the snow-mobiles?"

Again nothing.

"All right, make sure she can't get away. Same plan as before."

———

The early morning was dark, cold, and miserable. The snow was still falling, and the landscape appeared as though draped in a gray blanket. In the east, the dawn was still asleep and wouldn't wake for at least another few hours.

Wolf and I made our way along a deserted street, searching for any indication that someone else was about. We couldn't reach the outside world, but our comms was working, enabling us to talk to each other.

"Where do you figure they're at?" Wolf asked me.

"No idea."

Turning a corner, we made our first discovery. I forced Wolf back and we stepped back the way we'd come. "You figure he saw us?" Wolf asked.

"I don't know."

I peered around the corner. The figure was still pressed against an old stone wall, using it for shelter. Parked on the street were seven snowmobiles. I figured there to be two on each, which, meant we had fourteen assailants.

I brought my G36K up and sighted before firing. The figure fell to the pavement, and I waited for there to be a knock-on effect, but nothing happened. I said to Wolf, "Keep your head on a swivel."

We both moved forward, keeping close to the wall. The downed shooter was dead when we reached him. I grabbed up his radio and listened. I could hear communications flicking back and forth in French. "French mercenaries," I said to Wolf. "They're talking about—"

"What is it?"

"They've spotted Tag and Lion," I replied. I said into our comms, "Bravo Six, copy?"

"Copy, One."

"The X-rays have you under direct surveillance. I repeat—"

Suddenly, I could hear gunfire in the distance filtering through the storm. Then Lion's voice came to me, "Contact! Bravo One, we're taking fire."

"Where are you, Six?"

"East side of the village."

"On our way. Hold on." I then reached out to the others. "Bravo Five, copy?"

"Copy, One."

"Take Eight and head to the east side of the village. Our chaps are under fire. Move."

"Roger that."

I turned to Wolf. He was a big man with a beard that now looked white with rime. "Can you make these things go bang?"

"Does a bear shit in the woods?"

"Do it, then head back to the pub. Watch your six."

"Roger that, boss."

I moved as fast as I could toward the sound of gunfire. The snow made it tricky, but I made good time regardless, reaching an intersection of a cross street. Using an old stone building that had once been a candy store for cover, I peered around the corner and saw muzzle flashes further along. "Six, where are you?"

"We're pinned down inside an old garage," he replied.

I looked along the street and could see the pedestal signpost standing erect on the sidewalk. That had to be where they were. "Got you. I'm coming. Five, talk to me."

"Almost there, boss."

"Six and Seven are pinned down. Just look for the signpost. We need to clear the buildings opposite."

"If that's you ahead of us, then we're coming to you."

I turned and looked, seeing the two figures coming my way. "I've got you."

They stopped beside me, their breaths turning to vapor in front of their faces. "We need to move along the far side of the street and clear them out somehow."

Jock nodded his shaggy head. The man was a former Commando but had been in the private sector for a couple of years. "Let's do it."

Crossing the street, we moved cautiously along it, not wanting to tip our hand before absolutely necessary. Reaching the first building that we needed to clear, we stopped outside the door, and Jock reached inside his coat and pulled out a frag grenade. He was a man after my own heart. Jock grinned at me, and I nodded.

He pulled the pin and kicked the door of what had been a clothing store. No sooner had it crashed back than the grenade followed. Several seconds later, it detonated, the loud blast partially muffled by the noise of the storm.

We breached. Two shooters were down. The grenade had torn them up pretty good. We cleared the rest of the store but found no more.

It was then we realized that the shooting had stopped. I hurried across to a window and peered out. There was no movement on the street. I said, "Six, copy?"

"Roger."

"What can you see?"

"Nothing. After you hit that building, they stopped shooting."

"Did they come out and run?"

"Negative."

If they didn't go out the front, they must have slipped out the back. And if they did that…

I turned slowly to face the rear of the store.

CHAPTER 14

Two stun grenades bounced across the floor into the middle of the room. "Oh, shit. Get down!"

The detonations did what they were supposed to do. It knocked all of us for a loop, but this wasn't my first go-around. I managed to shake off the effects and crawl across the floor, looking for cover. The mercenaries came thundering in, opening fire.

Jock was the first man down. He caught a burst in his body armor, which disabled him. The next burst punched bullets into his skull. I let out a curse and fired back. One of the mercenaries fell, but another two took his place. "Wolf, Fletch, get your shit together."

"Fuck me, man."

More gunfire chased Wolf into cover. As he hunkered down, bullets chewed scars into everything they touched. I opened fire again with my G36, trying to give him covering fire. "Wolf, get the fuck out of there."

While I laid down what fire I could, I managed to drop another attacker. This was enough to force them back, and to get Wolf out of his precarious position. He crawled over to where I was sheltered. I said, "We need to get out of here while we can. Fletch, where are you?"

"Doorway."

"Right, go."

"What about Jock?" Wolf asked.

"He's done."

"You sure?"

"Yeah. But, if you want, you can go back out there and check."

"I'll take your word for it."

"Six, are you clear?"

"Roger that."

"Head back to the bar. We'll join you there."

Wolf and I pulled back out of the old store and disappeared along the street. Snow still fell but the wind had dropped a little. It was still very cold, and I was looking forward to getting into the warm bar.

When we reached the old pub, I barked orders to fortify our position. Sunshine looked at me and said, "Where is Jock?"

"Down hard."

"Shit."

"We got a bit of payback, but they'll be coming."

Fletch said, "Let me get into the place across the street. If they try to get in there, they'll get a surprise."

I stared at the big South African for a moment while I considered his request. Nodding, I replied, "Hound, go with him. Watch each other's backs."

They set off out the door, leaving the rest of us to discuss what to do next. Sunshine said, "We should post someone on the back door."

"Wolf."

"On it, boss."

"Everyone else, check your gear and ammo. We could be here for a while. What do we have in the vehicles?"

"A radio and some spare ammo," Tag replied. "Sat phone as well. I left it there because it was fucking useless in this weather."

"Get them. Anyone have any grenades?"

I was met with silence.

"Right, we improvise. Find me some empty bottles. We're in an old pub, so that should be easy enough. And a hose. Again, old pub, should have some beer lines. Then we drain some fuel into the bottles and make some Molotov cocktails. Better than nothing."

For the next twenty minutes, we worked tirelessly to get it done. By the time we were finished, we had a dozen bottles filled with gas and ready to go.

"Take some upstairs," I said to Tag. "You base yourself up there."

"Roger that, boss."

"Now we wait."

"Who were these people?" German asked.

"It's in the report," Knocker replied.

"I'm asking you."

"They were French mercenaries there after Pushkin. You see, with him dead, it narrowed the odds for the next Russian president if something should happen to Lash. They were playing a game within a game."

"So Fyodor...ah, whatever his name is—"

"Yeltzin," Knocker said.

"He hired a team of mercenaries to get Pushkin."

I watched Knocker nod. "In a fashion."

"What do you mean?" Holland asked.

"He hired more than one."

"More than one band of mercenaries?" German asked incredulously.

"That's right. We were lucky to get out of there alive."

"I do believe so."

They came for us just on the dawning of a gray day when the snow was starting to ease. It was Fletch who called them in. "Boss, I've got movement along the street. Our French friends are leapfrogging each other as they move forward."

"Slow them down by any means possible, Fletch."

"Roger."

We took up positions and waited for Fletch and Hound to engage from their position across the street. Moments later, they sent an opening volley with their assault weapons. Two of the French mercenaries went down in the first fusillade, the others scrambling to take cover before returning fire.

A withering fire began hammering against the windows across the street where our guys were shooting from. The situation changed rapidly when one of the mercs fired a 40mm grenade from a grenade launcher and blew the window apart.

The explosion across the road rattled the old pub where we were sheltered. I could hear Sunshine trying to raise Fletch and Hound but getting no response except static.

"Bollocks," I growled and headed toward the door. "Sunshine, take over."

An icy blast encroached on our warmth as I threw open the front door of the old pub. Taking a deep breath, I began to run across the street toward the damaged building where our team was supposed to be.

The interior was shattered. Both operators were down. Fletch was dead, a large splinter of glass buried deep in his throat. Hound had been hit hard, his head and left arm bleeding. He was also unconscious.

I said into my comms, "Bravo Two, Eight is down. Three is hit hard. Could have a head injury, not sure. Send—"

Another explosion rocked the building. This time the grenade was off target, but it still shook my world as I threw myself to the floor for cover. "Someone knock that fucking thing out," I snarled.

As I scrambled to my feet, I knew I needed to escape the bloody bullet magnet I was in. Leaning down, I grabbed Hound. He was a big man, but I was all juiced up, adrenaline coursing through my bulging veins. I picked him up and managed to get him across my shoulders. From there, I staggered to the door. "I'm coming over. Don't fucking shoot me."

I lumbered across the street through the snow with bullets cutting the freezing air all around me. How I made it without taking a bullet, I'll never know. Mrs. Jensen's boy was just lucky, I guess. I placed Hound gently on the floor. Looking around, I saw Lion. "Check him out. Where is Sunshine?"

"She and Wolf have gone after that grenade launcher."

"Out the back?"

"Roger that."

Collecting a Molotov, I headed out the back of the old pub into a narrow alley that provided rear access to the series of buildings. Immediately, gunfire was audible. I ran forward and found Sunshine and Wolf trying to breach the rear of the target building. "What's the hold-up?"

"Bastards have dug in," Sunshine replied.

"Then let's move them. Fucked if I'm standing around here all day freezing my bollocks off." I passed her my G36. "Hold this."

She took the weapon, and I dug into my pocket for the matchbook supplied by Wolf earlier. I lit the wick on the Molotov and threw it inside.

The fuel bomb exploded in orange spray and the ignition source scattered throughout the immediate area. Listening to their cries of pain, I stepped inside, catching sight of two figures engulfed in flames. When I opened fire, they dropped to the floor.

As I pushed farther toward the flames, the sound of more gunfire came from within, followed by shouts of what sounded to be concern. The French mercenaries were retreating.

Then something else happened. The ammo on the burning mercs started to go off. "Oh, shit."

I backpedaled out of there and into the alley. "Come on, time to go."

———

Regrouping back in the old pub, we did an ammunition check and then tried to decide on our next course of action. By my quick calculation, the mercenaries only had five men left. Which made our numbers even. We also had two dead and one wounded.

Sunshine pulled me aside and she said, "What are we going to do now, boss?"

"I'm trying to decide."

"The way I see it, we only have two choices," she replied. "We either go out there and find them, or we wait for them to come to us. If we go out, we could get ambushed. If we wait, they could blow the shit out of us. Not my decision to make. But you need to make one."

I looked around the bar. I gave a curt nod. "You are right. Tag, you're with me."

"Where are we going, boss?"

"Backing up. We're going to can these pricks once and for all."

"Do I get extra pay?"

"Yeah, I'll buy you a beer. Sunshine, see if you can get comms back up. We need to get the fuck out of here."

Leaving our warm sanctuary through the front door, we trekked along the street until encountering footprints in the snow. It was like tracking a herd of elephants along a deserted beach. Obviously, one was wounded because the trail of crimson was a stark contrast against the snow. Following the trail as it left the main street, we were led right and then left up another. As we continued, the snow kept falling and the wind started to rise again.

The street wended its way through an S-bend, then down a slope toward an old stone bridge spanning a small creek. The creek was choked with snow and the water was likely frozen.

The surface of the bridge was icy and hazardous as we crossed it, working hard to maintain our footing on the slope rising on the other side. There were more buildings ahead of us, one of which exhibited a fading sign advertising vacation accommodation.

We went a few more steps before I stopped Wolf. "What's up?"

I looked around me. The storm was starting to clear, the wind, which had picked up earlier, was now dropping, and the snow had stopped falling. "Get off the street."

Pushing right, we climbed over a low stone wall, taking cover at the corner of a double-floored building, and waited for a moment.

Peering around the edge of the building, I tried to detect any telltale signs of where the mercs might be. But there was none. Just their footprints in the snow along the street we'd just left.

"They're up there somewhere," Wolf said. "I can feel them."

"Probably watching us," I replied.

I raised my G36 and started to sweep the street and buildings. Meanwhile, back across the creek, a pall of dark smoke was staining the sky above the burning building we'd ignited with the Molotov cocktail.

"You see anything?" Wolf asked.

"Nothing," I replied. "Cover me."

I broke away from the building and started moving forward, half expecting a fusillade of fire or a sniper's bullet to take me out. But nothing happened. I sought refuge in a doorway and then waited for Wolf. He joined me a couple of minutes later before leapfrog-ging me and moving further along the street.

Again, there was refuge sought in a doorway and then I hurried to join him. "Anything?"

"Nope. Makes me wonder."

"Me too. Maybe they've pulled back out of town," I theorized.

"Only one way to find out," Wolf said.

I grabbed his shoulder. "My turn."

"Suit yourself."

Again, I broke cover and traversed further along the snow-covered street. And that was when what I'd feared earlier happened. A bullet hit me in my body armor, but it still put me down.

I felt like I'd been kicked in the chest by a horse, or what I thought that would feel like. The air left my lungs, and I fell onto my back. Wolf called out as he ran forward. The big man grabbed my clothing using one hand and dragged me into cover, bullets snapping all around him.

He kneeled beside me, checking me over. "I'm okay. Took it in my chest plate."

"Shit."

We were in the relative safety of a narrow walkway between two buildings. Groaning as I got to my feet, I looked out in the direction the shooting had origi-nated. They'd set up in a building a short distance along the street. It was set farther forward on the block than its neighbors, giving the occupiers a great field of fire.

"We can't go that way."

Wolf nodded across the street. "Maybe we could get a better approach from over there."

"Just what I was thinking. Give me some cover."

Wolf shook his head. "Nope, my turn."

My chest was still hurting. "Fine."

The G36 in my hands came up and I opened fire. Wolf broke cover from the laneway and ran across the street while I lay down a withering rate of fire to cover him. Barreling into a door on the other side, he broke through, the flimsy barrier providing little resistance to the big man. Once he was set, I followed him over.

Making it across without further incident, we hurried through the building to the rear door, taking time to reload our weapons and catch our breaths before heading out again. Apart from the snow and some detritus of the past, the rear alleyway was clear. Wolf and I started along it toward the building where the French mercs were holed up. We were halfway there when I stopped. Wolf looked at me. "What is it?"

"Can you hear it?"

"What?"

I looked up at the rapidly clearing sky. I opened my mouth to speak, but my words were lost in the rotor wash of a helicopter as it blasted overhead, followed by another two. When they were gone, I said, "Bollocks. We need to get out of here."

"Did you recognize them?"

"No."

"Let's have a look."

Shaking my head at how crazy the suggestion was, we turned and set off through the village streets in the opposite direction of the French mercs, and it didn't take long to reach the LZ. The last helicopter was disgorging its load. I counted twenty men forming a perimeter around the landing zone. All were dressed for winter combat. Wolf said, "I know one thing. They're not French mercs. Look at their weapons."

He was right. They looked to be armed with FN2000s. A compact Bullpup assault rifle. "Belgians."

"Yes, lots of them. There's only one guy I know of who would put that many in the field for a simple job like this."

"Who's that?" Wolf asked.

"Jan Casteels."

"Shit. Do you think he's with them?"

I shrugged. "Who knows? I hope he is so I can put a bullet between his eyes."

Wolf looked at me. "History, huh?"

"Something like that. About ten years back I'd been leading an SAS team in the Congo. We were doing jungle maneuvers when we were called in to observe some mercenary activity. It was rumored they were helping a mining company from South Africa relocate villagers off land they wanted to mine. They were relocating them all right. By putting them straight in the ground. After reporting back, we were ordered to stand down. Apparently, some British MPs had shares in the mine, and a blowup would be embarrassing for the government at the time."

"I'm guessing you didn't stand down," Wolf said with a grin.

"Affirmative. Hitting them as hard as we could, within ten minutes of the action kicking off, they were on the run. We didn't hang around, but the body count was twenty of theirs for zero of ours. Of course, when we returned to base, I was reprimanded and sent home."

"What happened to Casteels?"

"He got away with it."

"Now you figure he's here?"

"Yes, and we need not to be."

Falling back, we headed to the old pub. It was time to get the hell out of there.

CHAPTER 15

"WE'RE NOT GOING TO GET THE VEHICLES OUT, Knocker," Sunshine said to me, shaking her head. "Besides, Hound isn't in good enough shape to travel."

"I'll be fine," the big operator grunted. "Just get me pointed in the right direction."

"You have a concussion," Sunshine pointed out.

"Fuck the concussion."

She turned to me. "I advise against it, but I don't think we have much choice. What about our French bitch?"

"We either take her with us or put a bullet in her head."

"So, we're taking her with us then."

"I guess so. Get everyone ready."

Five minutes later, we left the pub via the back door and headed in the direction of a low ridge behind the village. The clouds were continuing to clear but we were still unable to make a connection to anyone.

Cresting the ridge, we climbed over a snow-covered stone wall, allowing for the slower rate of travel for our injured teammate. Beyond it were white squares where fields used to be, bordered by stark white powder-covered trees. I turned to Tag. "Stay here and watch our backtrail. I want to know what they're up to."

"Roger that."

"Catch up to us when you're done."

As we set off again, Wolf took point, crossing the first field and then skirting the second. Making use of the trees for cover, we progressed cautiously, just in case we were under observation. Having reached the far side, we took a five-minute breather to give Hound a break.

Tag caught up with us while we were resting. "They're coming. Looks like the Belgians and French together."

I nodded. "Break out the rifles."

We were carrying two Remington MSRs. They were both .300 caliber weapons. Each round left the muzzle at roughly 900 meters per second. It was a bolt-action weapon with a 7-round box magazine.

I took one and handed Tag the other. While the group set off after Wolf, Sunshine made sure Pushkin and the French woman kept moving. Tag and I settled down, hoping to thin the numbers of our pursuers.

My eye went to the Schmidt & Bender telescopic sight, and I focused on the ridge. Beside me, Tag did the same. A few minutes later, he said, "Knocker, I've got movement to the right of that gate at two o'clock."

I swung the rifle so I could see what he was talking about. At first there was nothing, then I saw the flicker of movement before picking out a person with a pair of binoculars. "He's looking for us."

"Yeah," Tag replied.

In front of us was a stone wall. We were using it to rest our rifles on. Our white battle smocks helped us to blend into the background, so seeing us was going to take some doing. Not that it was impossible.

The guy with the binoculars ducked back and then reappeared with someone else beside him. They were deep in discussion, and he seemed to be pointing in our direction. "You think they see us?" Tag asked.

"I guess we'll find out."

Moments later, a third person appeared. This one had a sniper rifle. He rested it on the stone wall they were sheltering behind and sighted in our direction.

I said to Tag, "Whatever you do, don't move or fire."

"Even if he's shooting at us?"

"I have a feeling that they're kicking the grass over to see what comes out."

"I hope you're right."

The first shot came, hitting the wall between us. The second shot was to my right and the third further right, confirming my theory. I said, "Just wait until they come over the hill."

The shooting stopped and we waited. It wasn't long before the mercenaries began pouring over the ridge. I said, "Just wait for a few more moments."

Tag and I watched as they kept coming. Tag said, "I'll start left, you start right."

"Sounds good to me."

We waited several additional moments, and I said, "Send it."

The MSR slammed back against my shoulder and my first target dropped into the snow. Beside me, Tag fired as well, and his target imitated mine. I worked the bolt and slammed home a fresh round.

Picking out another target, I fired again. This time, the merc was on the move and I only managed to wound him. However, getting hit by a .300 round wasn't like getting stung by a bee. He wasn't going anywhere in a hurry.

After Tag's next shot, the mercs went to ground. Returning fire from their prone positions, their weapons didn't carry the same range that our MSRs did, which was the best part of them being so far away.

Except for their sniper.

Ducking down behind the wall before the sniper could pick us as targets, I glanced at Tag and said, "Time to move. We'll split and then fire another shot each. Their guy will be looking for us now. Once we shoot, we go."

"Roger that."

We moved along the wall about twenty feet in opposite directions. Once we were set, I said into our comms, "On three, Tag."

"Roger."

"One...two...three..."

We each rose and brought the MSRs to rest in the snow atop the wall. I found a target starting to move and my crosshairs settled on him. I squeezed the trigger at the same time Tag did. Both bullets found their mark. The only issue was that we had chosen the same target.

We dropped back down behind the wall. Tag said into my ear, "Did we just shoot the same bastard?"

"Yeah, I think so."

"Shit."

"Let's go."

Tag crouched behind the wall as he walked toward me. From there, we kept moving until we reached the edge of the field where the trees were. We crossed the fence to put the trees between us and them before heading away in search of the others. We finally caught up with them on the far side of a rolling hill that bisected two more fields.

"We heard the shooting," Sunshine said.

"We only managed to slow them down, but it won't be for long. We need to keep moving."

Sunshine nodded. Overhead, the clouds were closing in again, and in the distance, it looked like it was starting to snow once more. I nodded toward the incoming weather. "We keep going that way."

"Into the storm?"

"Yes. With some luck, we'll lose them."

"But the nearest village is ten miles south of here."

"Yes, but they'll be expecting us to go that way," I replied. "We get into that storm, and then we swing south."

"You're the boss."

I took back my G36 and slung the MSR. "Let's go."

Cresting the next hill, an expansive valley lay before us, and we adjusted our direction to pick up a snow-choked stream surrounded by trees, snaking its way along the valley floor. We crossed the narrow waterway and began using the trees to cover our retreat. By the time we reached the end of the field, the snow was coming down hard again, even though the wind wasn't strong.

Stopping to rest beneath the trees before continuing, I ordered Lion back to watch our rear. After a three-minute break, when we were on our feet again, Lion reappeared. "They're still back there, Knocker."

"I figured as much. Let's keep moving."

For the next hour, we plodded steadily until we were fully enshrouded in the storm. I dropped in beside Sunshine and said, "It's time to turn."

"Copy."

Setting off in the direction of the village that was our goal, Pushkin and the French woman seemed to be traveling well. Once she had given the order, Sunshine came back to me.

"Have you tried the sat phone again?"

"Still the same."

"I can have a look at it if you want?" Tag said on his way past.

"What do you know about sat phones?"

"My brother was an electronics whizz. Some things rubbed off."

I shrugged and took out the phone. "Here."

"I'm going to need a few minutes."

I nodded. "Fine, Sunshine, pull them up again. Put Wolf on rear security."

"Roger that."

So, we waited again. This time for a shorter period than anticipated. When he was done, Tag asked, "Who cut the wire?"

"What wire?"

"There was a wire cut in it."

I raised my eyebrows. "Not broken?"

He shook his head. "No, not that wire. But don't worry, you should be able to use it now."

I looked around at the group before saying, "Don't mention it to anyone, Tag."

"Sure. You figure someone here isn't who they claim to be?"

"I'm almost certain of it. The problem is, who?"

"It could be any one of us," Tag pointed out. "Even you. Maybe Jock or Fletch."

"Well, we can't fucking ask them," I growled.

"No, we can't."

"Tell Sunshine to move everyone out. I've got a call to make."

I checked the phone was working before I dialed.

"Ray, where the hell are you?" Holly answered. "I've been trying to get you and—"

"Hold up, Holly, and I'll fill you in. We got stuck in the storm and took shelter on the way back. The thing was, Fyodor deployed mercenaries to find us. We're currently in a running battle with Jan Casteels."

"The Jan Casteels?"

"Yeah, that same bastard. We need an extract from a small village called Freetown."

"Is that where you are?" Holly asked.

"Not yet. We're headed there."

"Give me your coordinates, Ray."

"Won't do you any good, girl. We're in the middle of another blizzard. Once it lifts, we'll need that help."

"I'll get it to you somehow."

"Right, any news on Max Stiles?"

"We're working on a lead," Holly replied.

It suddenly dawned on me that she was speaking

loudly and there was noise in the background. "Are you in a helicopter?"

"Yes."

"What are you doing?" I asked her.

"We are following that lead I just mentioned," she replied.

"Copy. Watch your ass."

"I'd rather have you watching it."

"You'll be fine. Besides, your ass is too much of a distraction."

I heard her laugh. "I'll get that help you need, Raymond."

"Don't call me—" The call went dead.

I put the sat phone away and we continued to slog our way through the storm.

————

The direction we were headed took us over numerous undulating hills until we reached a valley with steep sides and a river running its length. Both riverbanks were lined with buildings. This was Freetown. Once a milling town from back in the eighteenth century, it had seen more changes than the maternity ward in a London hospital. Covered with white, the scene was picturesque, like something you'd see on a postcard. And down there somewhere was the local police station.

"Lion, take us in."

"Roger that."

The lower we went, the colder it became. The chill air settled in the valleys this time of year. We reached the outskirts of the village and followed a street across the river and into town proper. The police station was another hundred meters past the bridge. We'd almost made it when Tag said to me, "You notice something, Knocker?"

"What?"

"There is no one out and about."

"I'm not surprised, it's fucking snowing."

He nodded. "Yes, but it's not blowing. When I was a kid, I'd get out and play even if it was snowing."

"That just made you bloody crazy," I replied.

"Just wait here. I'll go and check."

"Fine."

Tag started forward and Sunshine came up beside me. "What's happening?" she asked.

"Tag is getting jumpy," I replied.

I watched as he drew level with the police station and started up the steps to go inside. He reached the stoop, opened the door, and froze. A heartbeat later, his head snapped back, and the report of a gunshot reached us. "Oh, shit. Get off the street!"

More gunfire erupted, but we were already moving. Bullets snapped through the crisp air all around us. I heard Hound cry out and then watched him fall. He hit the street and bright blood began spray-painting the snow around him, the carotid artery severed by a round. There was nothing we could do to help him.

Moments later, he was joined by the French woman.

We scattered on either side of the street. Sunshine and I, along with Pushkin, crashed through the door of a stone cottage. Lion and Wolf went in the opposite direction. "Three and Six, copy?"

"Copy, One."

"It has to be Casteels. Is there anyone in that place where you are?"

"Negative. I'm guessing they've rounded them up and stashed them elsewhere."

"Wait a minute," German interrupted. "We were led to believe that the incident at Freetown was a terrorist event."

"If you want to put them in that basket, then do that," Knocker replied.

I said, *"That was the official line. The head shed didn't want the civilian population to know that there were mercenaries on British soil fighting to seize a Russian from another mercenary force."*

"What happened to the civilians?"

"They were rounded up and forced into the church."

"The police?"

"They killed them," Knocker replied.

"We need to pull back," I said over my comms.

Retreat was not an option as we suddenly began taking fire from all directions. They'd sprung their trap, and we were stuck tight in it. Meanwhile, the snowfall had stopped and the clouds were starting to clear.

"Forget that idea," I said. "Dig in, conserve ammo."

Finding a window, I went to work. The gunfire ebbed and flowed, with us doing our best to conserve ammunition. It was about then that we lost Lion and Wolf to a rocket. It had to have been a fifty-fifty call on which building to take out with it, and we got lucky.

One instant, we were shooting from the windows, the next, we were knocked backward by the explosion across the street. After several moments, I scrambled to my feet, brushed off the shattered glass, and went back to the window frame. The building across the way was destroyed. There was no coming back from it.

"Sunshine, are you all right?"

"Yeah, One."

"Get Pushkin, we're getting out of here."

"Copy."

We headed out the back door and into a wall of heavy fire. It was enough to force us back inside and leave us trapped.

Sunshine said to me, "That was fucked, boss."

"We can't stay here."

I edged back toward the door. We were taking fire from three different areas. I pulled back and moved further into the room. Then I had an idea. "Sunshine, these things are joined, right?"

"The buildings? Yes."

I passed her my G36.

"What are you doing?"

"Hopefully nothing stupid," I replied and ran at the wall.

I guess I got lucky because when I hit it, the wall gave way, and I went right through it. Normally, without renovation, I guess the wall would have been stone, but it had been reworked and replaced by studs and plaster.

Picking myself up, I looked back at Sunshine. She shook her head. "As you Brits say, you're a right pillock."

I held out my hand and she gave me my weapon. "It's called improvisation."

"If you say so."

"Well, if you didn't like that, you're not going to like my next idea."

"What do you mean?"

"Do you still have one of those Molotov cocktails left?"

"What are you going to do?"

I grinned at her. "Start a fire."

"Bloody hell."

The building had a basement. It was cold, damp, and well-secured. Before descending into its depths, I lit the firebomb and threw it.

"You deliberately set fire to someone's property?" Holland was aghast.

"It's okay, I told them to send the bill to the government," Knocker replied.

"You what?"

"You're a dick," Knocker said.

The fire above us became intense, but with the level of dampness below, it never came down. There was also a vent that allowed air to be sucked in by the flames, fueling them but also giving us much-needed oxygen.

All we had to do was wait it out. Now, I'm not saying that it was easy, but it provided a slim chance of survival, as well as precious time.

As the fire began to abate, we made preparations to leave. It was then that we heard the voices. They obviously hadn't given up looking for us. We backed into a corner as someone above us knocked the burning floor in. It came down with a crash, throwing off bright embers and causing the flames to flare.

The three of us braced ourselves for a burst of gunfire, but it didn't eventuate. Instead, there was the sound of a low-flying helicopter followed by shouts of alarm. Then they faded away.

Sunshine looked at me and said, "What was that?"

"Help."

———

Flown directly to Lyon, Interpol had taken Pushkin into their custody, leaving us free to continue our mission.

That night, Sunshine and I waited in an East End café to meet our guest. It was almost closing time, and we were the only patrons sitting inside drinking coffee.

After showers at our hotel, we had changed our clothes to jeans, jumpers, and heavy coats.

Sunshine said, "You figure he'll be here?"

"Slick said he would. That's good enough for me."

"I hope he's right."

As usual, he was. Ten minutes later, our guest arrived. Walking up to the counter, he ordered a mug of coffee. When it was brewed, he paid with cash, then turned to leave and saw us. That was his opportunity to run, but he never took it. Besides, we had people outside who would have taken him down.

With an air of resignation, he walked over to our table and sat down. He gave us a brief smile. "You seem to have many lives."

"It was touch and go for a while," I replied.

He shrugged. "So, what now? Your MI6 takes me in?"

"No, not tonight. You wanted me to do your dirty work, Fyodor. You also sent your hired mercenaries after us to make sure. We lost a lot of good people."

"It was nothing personal. Just—"

The suppressed Glock I held under the table fired three times. Fyodor stiffened and then slumped sideways in death. Sunshine got up and left. Our work here was done, but there was still a long way to go.

German shifted his gaze to look at Holly. "That leads us to you, Miss Smith. Mr. Jensen mentioned about you going after Max Stiles. Was that still the case?"

Holly nodded. "Yes, at this point in time, I was still out of contact chasing Stiles."

"Then you better tell us about it."

"Yes, sir."

CHAPTER 16

"FOR THE RECORDING, WE ARE NOW MOVING BRIEFLY ON TO *the questioning of Agent Holly Smith and her pursuit of the fugitive, Max Stiles,"* German said. *"Does anyone have objections?"*

He glanced left and right, and when nobody spoke, he said, "Right, Miss Smith, if you please."

Slick got intelligence that placed Max Stiles at a quarry outside of London. We hopped on a Black Hawk to do some reconnaissance. I led a team of Global operators. Strike Team Asp. There were five of them, led by a tough-looking German by the name of Schultz. Formerly German special forces, he led his team from the front. The planning for the mission was carried out by both him and his team. They'd selected a landing zone one kilometer from the quarry. There was a large patch of woods that provided cover as we approached.

Once we cleared the LZ, Klink—that's what his men called him—put Johnson on point, and we followed in his wake. It took an hour to get to the quarry and into a position where we could survey the target area.

Klink settled down next to me as I looked through binoculars. "It looks sketchy."

I nodded. "There are four guards that I can see. Two vans. There could be others in that office building. What worries me is that if Stiles is to take action the way we think he will, he'll need to leave soon."

"What if it isn't the target?" Klink asked me.

I frowned. It was something we hadn't considered. All of us had concluded that the rally was the target. I said, "I'm listening."

"Ma'am, you assume that the target is the rally, but the only way that can be an issue is if they get close enough to fire on the people going into the stadium. Sure, you'll get a reasonable return for your efforts but not what they want."

"Then what do you think he'll do?"

"Drive around the streets and shoot anything that moves."

"Why would he do that?"

"Think about it, if they do it at the stadium, it's all concentrated in one place. Do it the other way, they could drive halfway across London sowing terror everywhere they go."

I could see what he meant. "What if you're wrong?"

Klink shook his head. "I'm not."

"Then we need to shut them down now."

"Yes, ma'am."

I took up my Heckler and Koch 433 and checked the magazine, making sure I had a round in the breech. Klink issued orders to his men, and we began to move. I was paired up with an operator out of Glasgow, a former para named Johnny Ellis. His handle was Pegasus.

With him in the lead, we traveled through the woods and down to the edge of the quarry. Once in position, we waited for the order from Klink. Pegasus had the guard closest to us in his sights but waited for the kill order.

Moments later, it came, and his suppressed weapon spoke, and the guard dropped. I heard him say into his comms, "X-ray down."

Pegasus came to his feet. "Follow me, ma'am."

He tracked forward toward a front-end loader, taking up position beside one of its large rear tires. Pegasus said to me, "Wait here, ma'am."

He started forward and was halfway across the open area when one of the van's doors slipped open with a WHAM, revealing one of the mounted miniguns. My eyes widened. "Shit."

Without thinking, I brought up my suppressed 433 and fired toward the opening. "Pegasus, get out of there!"

The minigun opened fire with its ripping sound. Rounds cut through the air, catching Pegasus in no man's land. Before he was shredded, I remember him looking back at me, his face full of realization. I can still see him.

With a shout of anger, I flipped my fire selector to auto and burned through a magazine, firing at the van. I ducked back to reload. Meanwhile, the minigun tore a storm through the loader. Fortunately for me, they have big engines and tires.

My comms lit up. "Alpha, are you okay?"

"Copy, Bravo, I'm fine. Bravo Four is down hard, though."

"I saw it. Just stay where you are."

"Roger."

Suddenly, I heard motors fire up and the vans started moving. "Bravo, they're making a run for it."

"I see that, Alpha."

The vans were quickly gaining speed and heading out of the quarry. Meanwhile, we still had shooters to contend with. I muttered a curse and began searching for targets, selecting one and sending rounds from my 433. The guy fell, and I watched to see if he would reappear. He didn't.

It took a further five minutes to secure the quarry. Once that was done, our next issue was the vans. And Stiles was still at large. I looked at Klink. "Call in the helicopter, we need to find those fucking vans."

———

The Black Hawk flew low over the landscape as we searched for the vans. The sky was an ominous gray, but unlike to the north of us, there was no snow. Nor was there any sign of the vans.

A second helicopter had been called in to retrieve the remains of Pegasus. His teammates, well aware of the risks involved with being a black op operator, remained stoic regarding his death. They must have compartmentalized it and moved on. Once the mission was complete, they would grieve in their own ways.

An hour after losing the vans, ISR picked one up on Wellington Street in Slough. "Ma'am, we're being redirected to intercept a target ISR has picked up," the pilot said to me over the intercom.

"Copy."

I felt the helicopter bank and make its turn. Looking across from me I saw the impassive face of Klink. He nodded, having heard the radio chatter. The others reloaded their weapons and prepared once more to meet the threat.

Klink said to me, "You should stay on the helicopter."

Shaking my head, I said, "No, I can take care of myself."

He gave me a serious look and then said over the intercom, "Put her down in front of the van. We'll take it from there."

The helicopter seemed to drop and turn sharply, making my stomach flip. It then flared and touched down on the street with a hard jolt. No sooner had this happened than Klink, Potter, Finister, and Grover were out, their weapons up, and walking toward the suddenly stopped van.

Myself, I was about twenty steps behind them. Strike Team Asp was taking no chances or prisoners. Not that I could blame them. They were already firing at the van by the time my feet had touched the asphalt.

Moments later, the van's sliding door was open and they were all calling clear. When I reached them, Klink turned to me and said, "All X-rays are down, ma'am. The target wasn't with them."

"Fuck. Is the minigun secure?"

"Yes, ma'am."

"Right. Bulldog, copy?"

"Copy, Alpha," came the reply from the operations room.

"I need a location on that second van."

"We're doing our best, ma'am."

"Well, do your fucking best faster," I snapped back.

"Ma'am—"

"I'm sorry, that was uncalled for. Please, do your best."

"Yes, ma'am."

I walked over to Klink. He looked at me and asked, "Any word on the other van?"

"They're looking."

"Any word on your other team?" Klink asked.

I filled him in on what I knew. "Have you had much to do with Jan Casteels?"

"Yes. He's a bastard."

"So is Knocker," I said.

He gave me a questioning look.

I grinned mirthlessly. "Knocker is one of the best operators I've worked with. Apart from Kane. If you were to ask me who was better, I wouldn't know, and I'd hate to have to live on the difference."

"I've heard about their exploits around Global," Klink told me. "They've reached legend status."

"From what I can gather, the whole team was pretty relentless. They took on more suicidal missions than anyone I've ever heard of. I'm surprised they didn't lose more people than they did."

Meanwhile, as we talked, police, ambulances, and members of the Specialist Armed Response Unit joined us. Word had been relayed from Police Command regarding our identities, ensuring that no one would kill us.

We had just started our explanation of the situation to the incident officer when the next call came in. "Alpha, we have the second van."

"Copy, Bulldog, send details to the helicopter."

"Roger, ma'am."

I looked over at Klink. "They've got it. Time to go."

The helicopter was already spinning up as we ran to it, and moments later, it was lifting off the street and skimming rooftops on the way to the next intercept.

———

"Where are we headed?" I asked the pilot.

"Brent," he replied.

"Are they headed to Wembley Stadium?"

"Not sure, ma'am," came the reply.

"Bulldog, do you have eyes on the van?" I asked.

"Yes, ma'am."

"Are they headed to Wembley Stadium?"

"Wait one, Alpha," the operator replied. "Alpha, unable to confirm at this time."

"Fuck." I thought for a moment. "Bulldog, I need a current ISR feed from Wembley now."

"Yes, ma'am."

I took up my iPad, and moments later, the feed came through. I studied it, tracked the van, and then zoomed in on the stadium. Then I looked up and stared at Klink while asking Bulldog another question. "What time does the rally start?"

"In sixty minutes."

I zoomed out and then saw what I'd missed the first time. "Wembley is the target. Get us over there now."

The Black Hawk banked sharply and dropped in height as it skimmed low across the rooftops toward Wembley Stadium. The men of Strike Team Asp readied their weapons for the imminent mission.

I checked my own. Over the comms, the pilot said, "We are two mikes out."

Closing the distance seemed to take forever. Then suddenly, a call came over our comms. "We're getting reports of gunfire at Wembley Stadium. There is an armed shooter situation. We're counting at least six men with automatic weapons plus the van with the minigun."

"Damn it, hurry this thing up. Get us there."

"We're doing what we can, ma'am," the pilot said.

Glancing down at my iPad, I could see the scene starting to unfold in real-time. People were running everywhere. I could see a shooter running through the crowd, firing at random. There were multiple bodies lying on the hard pavement. I started to feel sick at the sight.

The pilot said, "We are one mike out."

After what felt like an eternity, I felt the Black Hawk flare and then touch down with a bump. No sooner had the wheels touched the pavement when all the members of Strike Team Asp scrambled out. I followed in their wake.

Out in front, Klink started directing his men left and right. I heard him say over the comms, "Potter, you go that way. Finister, on me."

That left Grover, who turned and said to me, "This way, ma'am."

I followed Grover toward the van. It was stationary, so we figured that the driver must have abandoned it. The minigun had ceased to fire because there were no targets for its sensitive sensors, but it had already done its damage. I figure there were at least fifteen to twenty people down. The scene was devastating.

Grover remained in front of me and swiftly cleared the van, but there was no one inside. The driver had gone. Gunfire sounded in the distance from the roaming shooters. I followed close behind Grover as we went into the stadium.

There were people running in every direction, attempting to escape the certain death they feared was coming their way.

There were more bodies inside. Running onto the concourse, we saw cafés and a beer house. Ahead of us, we could still hear gunfire. A stream of humanity began running toward us. Suddenly, a woman among them stumbled and fell, sliding and leaving a trail of blood behind her.

"Shit," I muttered and took cover behind a column.

Grover had gone down on a knee and was trying to find a target. Seemingly from out of nowhere, someone tackled him, knocking him to the floor. "Oh crap."

Leaving cover, I ran across to the flailing pair. I grabbed the civilian and shouted at him, "Get off him, you cock! He's one of the good guys."

But the man was snarling like a rabid dog, fighting for his life. I ground my teeth and hit him with the butt of my 433. The man grunted and fell to one side. I helped Grover to his feet. "Thanks—"

WHAP!

A bullet blew in from somewhere unexpected and

slammed into his side. Grover went down hard, his face contorted as pain set in. I grabbed him by his webbing and dragged him to the column I had sought shelter behind. I sat him up. He already looked pale and pasty. "Hang in there, Grover."

"I—I'm good, boss."

"Bravo One, Three is down. WIA."

"How bad, Alpha?"

I looked at Grover, who was fighting the pain. "He needs attention, but there is nothing I can do at the—"

A shooter appeared and my hand went for my Glock in its holster. It came out smoothly, and I fired four times. The shooter jerked wildly before falling to the concourse floor. "Fuck."

"Alpha, are you still there?" Klink asked me.

"Yes. How many shooters are we dealing with?"

"Unknown. Leave Three where he is. We need to put the rest of these shooters down."

"Roger that."

I kneeled beside Grover, grabbed the handgun from his thigh holster, and forced it into his hand. "There, don't shoot yourself in the foot."

"I'll be fine, boss."

It was the last time I saw him alive. He was hit harder than we figured and died maybe a short time later.

Leaving Grover propped there, I ran along the concourse past a café and another bar. Drawing level with a betting booth, I saw another shooter ahead of me. An armed policeman, part of the security in place, had confronted him. They exchanged fire, and both men fell. I ran over to them. My immediate assessment told me the terrorist was dead. The policeman, however, was wounded in the leg. There was a lot of blood pooling on the floor, so I knew he was seriously hit. As I searched for something to stop the bleeding, he asked me, "Who are you?"

"MI6. Give me your belt."

Unbuckling it, he pulled it free and handed it to me. I slipped it beneath his leg and put the end through the buckle. As I tightened it as hard as I could, he emitted a groan of pain. "That should be right until someone comes to help. Just release it every now and then."

"Thanks."

I dragged him over to a wall and sat him up. Then I gave him his weapon. It was a G36. "Any of those bastards come this way, put them down."

"Yes, ma'am."

Pressing forward but trying to avoid people running past me, I made my way toward the gunfire. The scene was chaotic. This sort of thing just doesn't normally happen in the UK. Yet here it was, brought on by a Russian plan to defeat the west and become the glorious nation it had once been.

Not too far ahead of me, I could see the back of another assailant. He was aiming his weapon at a young man desperately trying to flee. Someone was watching over that young man because it proved that the weapon was empty, and the gunman had to take precious time to reload.

My suppressed 433 came up and snapped into line. I didn't worry about giving the killer a warning. There was no point, and I was far from feeling forgiving. I fired three times, and he fell to the concourse floor. The young guy brushed past me as he sprinted in panic. I ignored him and walked over to the downed shooter. He was choking on his own blood.

I could have left him there to die just as he was, but instead, I drew my Glock again and put a merciful bullet in his head.

Suddenly, ahead of me, my line of sight cleared. The wave of panicked people had cleared and there was nothing else. Yet I could still hear gunfire. "Bravo, report."

"Alpha, we have multiple shooters on the first and second concourses."

"Where on the first?"

"Club Wembley East."

"On my way."

"Watch yourself."

"Copy."

More bodies were strewn haphazardly across the concourse floor. Some of the wounded were being helped by others. A few looked at me and started with fear. "It's okay," I said. "I'm Security Services."

That seemed to do the trick, but I knew that if a shooter got past me coming the other way, they were doomed.

The gunfire grew louder, and ahead, I could see another terrorist engaged with Klink. I brought my weapon into line and fired. The shooter's flank was wide open, and I had a clear line of sight. My first bullet took him in the side, hammering through flesh and finding the gap between ribs. I saw him stagger and fired again. This time, the round scrambled the bastard's brains and he died immediately.

A second terrorist appeared, looking in my direction. He opened fire at me, forgetting about Klink. His bullets hammered into a column I was sheltering behind and gouged large chunks out of it like a woodpecker.

However, the fatal mistake he made was forgetting about Klink because the German fired a long burst at him, and he died a violent death.

Klink called over to me, "Alpha, are you good?"

"I'm fine. What do we have left?"

"I think we're clear."

"What about Stiles?"

The German shrugged. "No idea."

"Bulldog, I need a location on Max Stiles," I said hurriedly. "And I need it yesterday."

"Ma'am, we have no idea where Stiles is. We'll run facial rec, but it could take a while."

"I don't care. Fucking find him."

"Yes, ma'am."

"Now, where is Pridham?"

"He's been evacuated by his people."

"Roger that." I turned and looked at Klink. "They have no idea where Stiles is."

CHAPTER 17

"THAT'S IT FOR STILES?" GERMAN ASKED.

"For me, it was," Holly replied. "It was Ray who tied that package."

"By tied, you mean —"

"Terminated the problem."

"When did this happen?"

"The day after the election. We couldn't find him until then."

German nodded. "Okay, let's pick it up from there. Mr. Jensen, continue."

"He's going to win," Holly said to me as she entered the ops room. "The bastard is actually going to win, and he's pressing for an emergency handover so he can get on the front foot and fix everything."

"Can he do that?" I asked her.

"Apparently, he can. I've been talking to an insider. The British troops abroad are on standby to withdraw as soon as he takes power. Kane thinks the Russians are going into Finland."

"Not Poland?" I asked.

Before I could answer, a head popped into the ops room. "Turn on the news. Things just ratcheted up a notch."

The large screen on the wall came to life and we got our first view of what was now going on in the east. Reaper had been right. The Russians were rolling across the frontier into Finland. More troop ships were sailing to Helsinki, and the capital appeared to be in utter chaos. I shook my head. "Ah, shit. It looks like Reaper was right."

Moments later, Holly was speaking to Kane on the phone. When she hung up, she said, "He's headed to Finland. Helsinki, actually."

"I hope he knows what he's doing."

"So do I."

Before we finished speaking, a call came through from Slick. Max Stiles had been located. Holly looked at me and said, "I need you to be at your worst, Ray."

"I wasn't planning on being anything else, boss."

"Good. Find him. Kill him."

———

Stiles was sequestered away in a club run by Benny Hagen, a criminal best known for extortion rackets and selling drugs for spare change. The club was Men Only and catered for all walks of life: Judges, lawyers, crooks, police, and your average bum off the street. Providing you had money, you were welcome at Benny's place.

The plan was to go in on my own, unarmed. If and when I needed a weapon, I knew I would be able to put my hands on one. Hagen's crew always went armed.

The building was a large colonial, standing three floors high, with many rooms spread on each. As I went inside, I immediately got the early 1900s vibe. All the male staff were liveried in white tuxedos. Which is more than can be said for the women who were scantily clad in panties and corsets trimmed with lace. As I crossed to the guy behind the reception desk, I said to him, "I'm here to see Benny."

"Mr. Hagen is very—"

WHAM!

I punched him in the mouth before he could finish. He went down like a sack of shit and rolled onto his side, moaning. I walked behind the counter and dragged him to his feet. "I wasn't asking. Now, where is he?"

"I think he is in the main service room," the man managed, wiping his bleeding lips with the back of his hand.

I grabbed my cell and showed him a picture of Stiles. "What about this bastard?"

"I—I think he is in one of the rooms upstairs."

"Which floor?" I asked.

"Second."

Releasing him, I said, "Go home, you look unwell."

Moving toward the wide staircase, I took in the dark wooden balustrades and steps lined with carpet the color of red wine. Meanwhile, behind the desk, my close personal friend had just triggered a silent alarm. I'd half expected it.

However, the silent alarm, in this case, was inter-house, not to the police. I hadn't even reached the top of the stairs before the first security guard appeared with his weapon drawn. "Hold it there, mate."

I turned around to face the man at the bottom of the stairs. I raised my hands and gave him a frustrated stare. "What now, mate?"

"Just come back down slowly."

The guard was soon joined by a second person and a third. The third being Hagen. He glared at me and growled, "Who are you?"

"The name is Jensen. I work for the Security Services."

"Five or Six?"

"Does it matter?"

"No, I don't suppose it does. Not where you are going."

"I couldn't ask you to reconsider?" I asked.

Hagen grinned. "Really?"

"I'm here looking for one man. I'm going to reach into my pocket for my phone and I'll show you a picture."

"I don't really care," Hagen snapped.

My hand kept moving anyway. It went into my pocket and then slowly reemerged. "Oops, wrong pocket."

They froze. With my left hand held high, they couldn't miss the fragmentation grenade I was holding. "Okay, this is what's going to happen. You on the left, walk toward me and give me your gun."

Although I was holding the grenade, the tall man dressed in white wasn't quite sure what to do in such a situation. He glanced at his boss and then back at me before moving up the stairs and handing me his H&K SPF9.

I took it, nodded my thanks, and then shot him in the head before doing the same to the man at the foot of the stairs next to Hagen.

"You just committed cold-blooded murder," Holland stated.

I glanced at Newman, who was still sitting quietly. He nodded as if to say, well done. My gaze then cut back to Knocker, who stared at Holland before saying, "At that point, we were beyond niceties. These people had brought war to my doorstep, and this asshole was hiding one of them. If you're not prepared to do what it takes, then you shouldn't be in the game."

It finally became clear why Holly had chosen Knocker for that specific job. Holland, however, still wasn't done. He turned to Christine Ryan and said, "Do you accept this?"

"That's what makes him the top operator he is," she replied.

"I cannot accept that. The details will be passed on to police once these hearings are done."

"I thought this was just a debrief?" I said.

"I think we should just continue," German said, interrupting.

Knocker said, *"Maybe if Holland can't stomach what happens in the real world, he should piss off. Because he isn't going to like what happens next."*

"Please continue, Mr. Jensen."

Hagen was shocked at what he'd just witnessed. But I didn't care. To me, he was as bad as the man he was harboring. "Where is Max Stiles?"

"Upstairs. Second floor."

"Show me."

"I—"

"Now."

Climbing the stairs toward me, he turned his back on me as he stepped past, as though my proximity would somehow taint him. I followed him onto the landing and then along a hallway lined with dark wood paneling and hand-painted originals on the walls. I said to Hagen, "You should have stayed home today."

"The police will be here very shortly."

"No, they won't. Most of your clients don't need the publicity, and for that matter, neither do you."

We'd walked almost to the end of the hallway when Hagen stopped outside a door on his left. "In there."

"Open it."

Nodding resignedly, Hagen reached for the door handle, his fingers brushing the metal lever as a string of bullets punched through the door. Misshapen bullets hammered into Hagen's chest along with long slivers of wood. He staggered back into the wall behind him, looking down at his torso, then slid gradually toward the floor where he came to rest.

Sometimes life sucks. Other times, people get what they deserve. I kicked the door and stepped to one side as more bullets exploded through the opening. I waited for a moment, then entered to see Stiles reloading his weapon, standing in the center of the room.

Glancing up, he saw me standing there and instantly dropped his weapon and raised his hands. "Don't shoot."

My eyes narrowed and I said, "Too fucking late, mate."

Then I shot him.

That night, for the first time in a while, I slept in my own bed. We were waiting for actionable intel, and my body needed to rest. Reaper was off doing his thing, and the first of the riots had started on London streets, with our new PM informing the public and his law enforcement officers to leave them alone because it was their right to protest.

Me, I didn't give a fuck either way. I needed to recharge for the next part of my mission. Meanwhile, Holly was working furiously behind the scenes, putting together a meeting with some very important people.

With all the attendees locked in, the meeting was scheduled for early the next morning. There would be five government officials as well as the heads of MI5 and MI6. I was sound asleep when Holly called me. "It's all set up. I need you in at eight. Can you do that?"

"I'll be there. Have you heard from Reaper?"

"No."

"If that's all, I'm going back to bed."

I was about to do just that when Holly said, "You know this ends only one way, right?"

"Yes."

"I won't order you to do it, Ray. This is entirely your decision."

"Seems like it is all we have, boss."

"I'm sorry."

"Don't be. Let's see what happens in the morning."

"Just to clarify, Mr. Jensen, what exactly were you talking about with Miss Smith?"

"Are you sure you want to know?" Knocker asked him.

"Yes, please elaborate."

"We were planning on assassinating Fergus Pridham."

"Now I've heard it all!" Holland exploded. *"This is —"*

"Mr. Holland, if you don't mind," Christine Ryan snapped. *"Why the hell are you here?"*

"I was asked, just like you."

"Maybe they shouldn't have. Let's continue. There isn't much left to go."

The next morning, when we arrived at Whitehall, everybody else was already there. John Lester, the outgoing PM. Morris West, the Chancellor. Guy Wilson, the Foreign Secretary. And Molly Porter, the Home Secretary. Joining them was Frank Travis, the deputy opposition leader who was to be sworn in the next day. You can also add to the list the heads of MI5 and MI6.

When we entered the room, every eye turned to us.

"Sorry for interrupting," German said, *"but where was Miss Ryan at this point in time? After all, she was your superior."*

"She was on her way back from Berlin," Holly supplied.

"So, she had no idea about this meeting?"

"No."

"Thank you."

Without delay, we were introduced to everyone and started from there. Holly spoke first. "Lady and gentlemen, I asked you here today to discuss a major threat to our national security. I guarantee you will not like what you are about to hear, but I assure you that every fact we are about to give you is true. If you open the folders in front of you, you will see that we have been working on this for some time."

"If you have been working on this for a while, why haven't I heard about it?" John Lester asked.

"It was thought best to keep it under wraps until there was no other way to proceed or that you needed to know. The only person who knew is the Home Secretary."

This wasn't quite true because Anesha Perera knew, and there might have been another. I'm not sure, nor do I care.

The PM looked at Molly Porter. "You knew?"

"Yes, sir."

He held himself in check and said, "Then you'd better tell me."

Holly continued, "Sir, this all started with a gas strike in Syria."

"I knew about the gas strike," Lester said as though he wasn't totally devoid of intel.

"We then uncovered a plot put in place by five Russian Generals, photos of whom are in the file. Initially, we were unable to identify them, but over time we've been able to put them all together and take a few off the chessboard."

"You mean you've killed them?" Frank Travis asked incredulously.

"Yes, sir."

He gave us a querying look. "Why isn't Fergus here?"

"We will get to that, sir, if you would just bear with us."

"Fine, but I don't like it."

"Neither do we, sir," Holly replied. "At this point in time, there are still three of the old generals left."

"What do you propose to do with them?"

"Eliminate the threats, sir."

"I see."

"May I continue?" Holly asked.

"Yes, please do."

"We followed the link from Syria to Congo, and then to Berlin where we—"

"Wait," Guy Wilson said. "That issue in Berlin that was called a terrorist action, was that you?"

"Most of the things that have happened recently are tied to us."

He nodded somberly.

"While we were in Berlin, a new threat became clear to us," Holly continued. "Nuclear missiles left over from the Cold War and the Cuban Crisis. We have neutralized that specific threat but, as yet, haven't been able to stop President Lash."

"Lash is part of this?" Lester asked.

"Yes, sir. A very large and integral part of it. He and the Generals were behind the assassinations of several people, which made it possible for him to rise to power and implement what we are now seeing."

"Good God."

"But it doesn't stop there," Holly told them. "We came across some code names while we were working on all of this. One is Hecate, and the other is Dolos."

"Who are they?" Wilson asked.

"Hecate, we are reasonably sure, is a mole in the intelligence services."

"And the other?" Lester asked. "This one called Dolos?"

I watched as Holly glanced at Molly Porter. The Home Secretary said, "Dolos, sir, is Fergus Pridham."

"Preposterous!" Travis exploded and lurched to his

feet. "I have never heard of anything so absurd in all of my life."

Holly said, "Sir, in your folder, you will find two pages outlining what we have on him. If you take the time to look through it, you will see that it is true. Also, we managed to get some pictures of him with a man named Oleg Zhirkov. Please, take your time."

I got up from the table and walked over to the window. Holly joined me. "Well, they haven't thrown us in prison, yet."

"I guess that's a start, boss."

There was movement beside us and we turned to face the Home Secretary. "I hope to God that they see this for what it is. If not, then I have no idea what to do next."

"We have a contingency," I said to her.

She cocked her head to one side and stared at me with dark eyes. "Tell me you are kidding, Mr. Jensen."

I shrugged. "Anything for King and Country, ma'am."

"For crying out loud." She stared at me for a moment, then said, "That's your only plan, isn't it?"

"Yes, ma'am."

"Fuck."

We returned to the table, and Lester looked up at us. "This is unbelievable. How could something like this happen?"

"They are that good, sir. Right now, they are invading Finland, which is part of their plan. We think that Poland will be next."

"I still cannot believe that Fergus is part of this."

I said, "He is the one wanting to bring our troops home, withdrawing help from NATO. The US aren't moving because we aren't. We have the two biggest parties doing nothing, and Russia will do as it wants. This is why he wants the urgent changeover."

"The people have spoken," Travis pointed out.

"Yes, because he helped unleash a wave of terrorism on our shores, which benefited him."

Holly then put her two cents' worth in. "Sir, we have been able to link them to an MI6 operative in Moscow, a financial terrorism expert from MI5, and the bomb that killed Winston Jones."

Travis glanced at the two silent security bosses. "Is this true?"

They both nodded.

"Oh, shit. What are you proposing that we do?"

Holly hesitated. After all, it wasn't every day that you proposed to assassinate a high-ranking politician. Instead, I took over. "We are trying to find Zhirkov, who we believe is still in the country. When we do, we will take him off the board like the others."

"What about Fergus Pridham?" Lester asked.

"Sir, to save the country the embarrassment of a public trial and the circus that comes with it, I propose that we terminate him with extreme prejudice."

"What?" Travis blurted out. "You can't just assassinate a man with such political standing. That makes us like them."

"I realize that, but what I'm proposing is the best option. The only option."

They all stared at me before Lester said, "Please give us a minute while we discuss options."

"Yes, sir."

"Oh, before you go, Mr. Jensen, I do know your reputation, what you have done for this country. We will give your suggestion a great deal of consideration."

"Thank you, sir."

Leaving the room, we went off to find Slick. Just down the corridor a way, Holly said to me, "What's your read?"

"They won't go for it."

"That's what I was thinking too."

Locating Slick, he was hard at work as usual, his fingers dancing over his keyboard. My first question to him was, "Have you found Reaper?"

"No, I've heard nothing."

"What about Zhirkov?"

"Nothing yet, but he won't be far away." Slick hesitated. "What about the meeting?"

"No outcome yet, but they're discussing their options."

"I see."

We were called back less than ten minutes later, and we entered the room where some of the select group looked confident, and others appeared uneasy at the decision reached.

Lester spoke first, "We have decided that you should find Oleg Zhirkov and deal with him. As far as Fergus Pridham is concerned, he will be dealt with through the proper channels."

Holly glanced at the Home Secretary who was one of those looking less than happy. "Sir, this is not the time to be playing politics. He will be sworn in tomorrow, maybe the next day, and then he becomes virtually untouchable. That leaves the country at the mercy of him and his masters."

"I note your concerns, but I will do my best to delay the inevitable."

I looked at Travis. "What do you have to say?"

"We live in a democracy. We can't commit a coup—"

"Coup my fucking ass," I growled. "The only coup here is the Russian government taking over our own. Fucking pillock."

"That will do, Mr. Jensen," Jackson, the head of MI6, said softly.

I turned on him. "Sir, you know what I'm saying is true."

"Yes, but my hands are tied."

"Bloody hell."

Lester nodded. "All right, that's it. Thank you all for your time. Mr. Jensen, Miss Smith, please remain for a moment."

Three of the attendees filed out, leaving Lester, Jackson, Pettigrew—the new boss of MI5—and Molly Parker.

Lester gestured with his hand and said, "Please, take a seat."

Holly and I looked at each other before sitting.

"What we are about to discuss will be deniable on all levels."

"Something we're used to, sir," Holly replied.

"You have authority to do whatever it takes to stop Fergus Pridham," Lester said.

"Whatever it takes, sir?" I asked.

He nodded.

Jackson said, "We can't have a foreign power get its

claws into us like this. So, we must eliminate the problem."

"What if I get caught?"

"Don't."

It was a stupid question. "What happens once it is done?"

"We will cross that bridge when we get to it. The truth of his complicity in all of this will eventually be revealed, but we feel that it is best to eradicate the problem now."

I nodded slowly.

Lester said, "We have no right to ask you to do this, but…"

"It's okay, sir," I replied.

"Sir," Holly said. "You need to be aware that Pridham doesn't just have normal security. His are specially trained operators from the new KGB. They are all conversion school graduates where they learned every detail about our way of life, as well as taking English lessons, the result of which makes them hard to differentiate from us. If we're going to do this, we need to get him out of London so we have a free hand away from prying eyes."

"I think I can get that organized," Molly said. "Leave it with me. Is tomorrow too soon?"

"Tomorrow will be fine," I replied.

"I can't believe we're actually doing this," Lester said softly.

I stared at him. "You're not, sir, I am."

He nodded. "Yes. Oh, there is one thing. What if you miss?"

"I'll be dead."

"Good luck, Mr. Jensen."

CHAPTER 18

German looked at Knocker stoically. "*The PM unofficially sanctioned the assassination of a member of Parliament? Is this true?*"

"*Just remember, this guy wasn't on our side,*" Holly told him.

"*But still—*"

Knocker said, "*If I can keep going, I think I can muddy the waters a little more.*"

"*Don't you mean clarify?*" Holland asked.

"*Clarify, be fucked,*" Knocker growled. "*This is my world. Nothing is ever clear.*"

It wasn't until the next morning that word came through. There was to be a meeting held that afternoon at Tarrant Estate outside of London, where Pridham was to meet with certain people from the current administration to discuss the hurried transfer of power.

It was a ruse of course. All communications in and out of the estate had been blocked, and once the small cavalcade passed through the iron gates, the bollards went up, and there was no going back.

I was already there. The interior of the mansion was made up of a warren of hidden passageways and doors. I had studied them in depth and committed them to memory. Except for the one room where the meeting was to be held. That was a sealed area with only one entry.

We could have used a team, but prudence had us deciding against it. The more people who knew would greatly increase the chance of a leak. So, I was Robinson Crusoe.

Pridham had brought a nine-man security team with him, all armed with automatic weapons. Mostly MP5s. It appeared as though they were guarding a crime boss rather than the incoming PM. Nothing about them was covert.

Once Pridham was inside, I said to Slick, "Block any outgoing transmissions but keep our line open. I don't care if they talk to one another because once this kicks off, any panic helps me."

"Copy, Bravo."

"And remember, no names."

"Roger that."

With those final instructions given, I went to work and did what I do best.

"Two in the hallway, Bravo."

Stepping from the room I was in, I was confronted by two men near the doorway. My suppressed Glock came up, and I fired at the first security man. His head spasmed as my bullet plowed into it, and he died immediately, crashing to the floor. My aim changed and the Glock fired twice more. The recipient of those rounds was reacting to the death of his compatriot and flailed wildly before joining the other man on the floor.

"Bravo, go along the hallway and through the door. It's all clear on the other side."

Without responding, I followed the instructions. Opening the door, I found myself in another long hallway. It was lined with flocked wallpaper and artwork depicting hunting parties on the walls. Stretching out ahead of me was a long red carpet hall runner that matched the patterned colors of the wallpaper. At the end, beside a large oak door, was a potted plant with shiny green leaves.

I continued moving steadily toward the next door but stopped halfway along and turned left through another. This one was a drawing room, and I hurried across to a large bookcase. On the second shelf was a hefty tome, which I reached for and pulled back.

With an audible snick, the bookcase moved, so I pushed it open far enough to squeeze through the gap. Closing the manufactured door behind me, I took out a flashlight and made my way through the narrow passage built between the walls. When I reached the end, I paused in front of another secret doorway. "Alpha?" I whispered.

"Room is clear."

The hidden door was a large plain panel in the wall. The carpentry was so good that it was impossible to differentiate it from the other wainscoting, so most people didn't know it was there. I pushed it closed behind me and walked toward the door. I was in another drawing room.

"You have another shooter roaming the hallway

beyond the door, Bravo," Slick said. "I'll tell you when."

So, I waited, and then his voice filled my ear. "Now."

Opening the six-panel door, I saw the shooter walking away from me. The Glock was already up and all I had to do was fire. Which I did.

Entering the back of the well-dressed man's head, the bullet felled him like a tree.

"Bravo, behind you!"

The urgent warning made me pivot and drop to a knee. My suppressed Glock spat another round, and the man who was about to shoot me died with a surprised expression on his face.

"Thanks, Alpha," I whispered.

"Go through the doorway he just came from, Bravo. Be aware there is another on the other side."

Heading toward the door, I paused when Slick said into my ear, "Wait, Bravo."

I could hear footsteps on the other side.

"Wait…"

"Wait…"

"Wait…"

My hand rested on the door handle.

"Now."

I turned, pushed, and stepped through. The security man was walking away and never got to turn around before he was dispatched on his way north with his comrades. Or maybe it was south.

Slick said, "Okay, along the hallway, take the door on your left. You should find the next secret passage behind the grandfather clock."

I followed his directions, despite my prior knowledge. It was one less thing for me to think about. Pushing open the door, I walked across the room to the beautifully ornate clock. Opening the glass door, I pulled the pendulum chain.

Something clicked, and I was able to access the hidden door. Before entering, however, I closed the glass front on the clock, making sure I had left no finger smudges that might give away my presence.

This hidden hallway was longer than the last. It led me between unpainted walls and opened into a large ballroom area. As I made my way along it, Slick said to me, "Pridham is getting nervous. You need to speed things up."

Reaching the door to the ballroom, Slick informed me that it was clear. He said, "Leave through the east door, which will take you along the internal walkway bordering the internal garden."

The internal garden was effectively a large greenhouse. It was filled with tropical plants, and the artificial environment kept growing perfectly. I was about through when I heard Slick say, "Danger close."

Leaving the walkway, I entered the dense foliage and crouched down. Drawing my combat knife, I waited, hearing the door squeak open. The sound of approaching footsteps could be heard. My grip tightened on the knife.

As the figure drew closer, I held my breath to remain as silent as possible.

Then, the shooter was level with me, and I acted, springing toward him and killing him silently with my knife. Looking around guiltily, I pulled his body into the garden, trying to do as little damage as possible so it wasn't obvious that anyone had been there.

With that done, I moved on.

Slick informed me the rest of the bodyguards were in the large dining hall with Pridham. "You need to move faster."

"Shut up. I'm bloody there."

The double doors flew back, and all eyes turned on me. One look from Pridham and he knew why I was there. "Kill him!" he screeched.

My Glock spoke rapidly, and the first bodyguard fell, a bullet in his face. Before he touched the slate floor, the second one was on his way to join him. Number three got off a shot but was too panicked to shoot straight. His round punched through a dark wood panel on the wall behind me. My bullet never missed.

Three down.

That left Pridham. He backed away from me, his mouth opening and closing like a fish. "Hello, Fergus."

"Wh-what are you doing?"

"I think you know," I replied in Russian. "I'm here to pass judgment."

"What? I don't know what you mean?"

"Fuck off, Dolos."

That got his attention. He looked shocked, then angry, then a string of words tumbled from his mouth in Russian. "You cannot stop us. Mother Russia will be great again."

"Your plan is fucked," I snapped at him. "The missiles won't do any good, the generals are going to be killed, and Lash is going to hell right along with them."

"You—"

I shot him. There was no more to say. "Alpha, send in the cleaners."

———

Later that day, Holly and I met with John Lester. His expression was grim but somewhat relieved when the news was broken to him. "So, it is done."

"Yes, sir."

"Thank you, Mr. Jensen. Your country thanks you."

"We're not done yet," I reminded him.

"You'll have to take that up with the new PM."

"Who might that be, sir?" Holly asked.

There was a knock on the wooden door behind us. Lester said, "Here they come now."

When the door swung open, a woman walked in. Lester said, "I'd like you to meet Miriam Craig."

Miriam Craig was tall, slender, and had dark hair. She was my age and about to become the youngest PM the UK had ever had. And—

"Hello, Raymond."

I knew her. Intimately.

"Really?" I said to Knocker, interrupting his dialogue. "Is there anyone you haven't slept with?"

"Ex-wife," he replied.

"Shit. How many women were you married to?"

"Too many."

"Hello, Miriam. I see you never let life hold you back."

"You know her?" Holly asked, turning to look at me incredulously.

Before I could reply, Miriam said, "We were once married."

"Christ, how many times were you married?"

"Too many."

Miriam sat down. Lester said, "We were just discussing next steps. I told them they would have to clear it with you."

"The Home Secretary brought me up to speed," Miriam said. Her hawkish eyes focused on mine as though it was all my fault. "I can't believe that this has been happening under our noses."

"Believe it," I said. "We've been fighting them every step of the way since we found out about it."

"Well, thank God for small mercies is all I can say," she replied. "You might have been a shit husband, Ray, but as an operator, you left nothing on the table."

"Thanks, I think."

"So, where to from here?"

"Ma'am," Holly said. "We're still trying to locate Oleg Zhirkov to…"

"Kill him?"

"Yes, ma'am."

"Fine. I have no qualms about that."

"We also have a man in the field headed to Helsinki to locate another of the Russian generals. His name is Genady Morozov."

"The man in the field? Who is he?"

"John Kane, ma'am."

"Your friend, Ray?"

"Aye."

"Then I pity the poor man. What else can you tell me?"

"It is probably best that we don't tell you, ma'am. Plausible deniability and all," Holly said.

I glanced at her, trying to catch her gaze to warn her off. All to no avail.

"Miss Smith, I will decide what I do and don't need to know. Not you." Her tone stirred up a whole cauldron of memories.

"Yes, ma'am."

"Well?"

Fuck it. "The ultimate goal is to assassinate Sergey Lash," I replied.

"The current president of the USSR?"

"That's right."

"Wrong. His death will create a vacuum—"

"Fuck the vacuum." I was talking to my ex-wife now, not the new PM. Yes, it was wrong, but I'd heard that tone too many times. "Listen, Miriam, we have someone who will step into that void once Lash is gone."

"You mean replace him with one of ours?"

I shook my head. "He's far from one of ours. You can meet him and decide for yourself."

She nodded. "I shall. I'm still not happy with assassinating the leader of a foreign country. If at all possible, can you take him alive?"

"I'm not going to promise you anything, Miriam," I replied.

"Same old Raymond."

"Let us deal with the mechanics, Miriam. You take care of the country. I'd say right now, you have your hands full."

"You're right. Right now, I have SAS, SBS, and Commandos all deploying along with four squadrons of aircraft to bolster the NATO air wing. The Americans are working through logistics and will be in a position to help soon."

"Meanwhile, Helsinki is a battleground."

"Yes."

"Then we'd better get back to work."

"Something has happened to John," Holly said to me.

"What?"

"I don't know, but we're sure the Russians have him."

"Bollocks, get me on a plane," I growled.

"No, I need you here."

"I need to find Reaper," I told her.

"It is believed that Zhirkov is still in the country and we have a lead."

"Where?"

"Norwich," she replied.

"Where in Norwich?"

"We're not sure. Slick found a link between Zhirkov and an old man, an immigrant. He came from Russia in the nineties."

"So?"

"He is the boss of the Russian mafia in the Norwich area," Holly told me. "His father was KGB and personally knew Zhirkov."

"Doesn't mean he's there," I pointed out.

"No, but he might know where he is. We have a helicopter waiting to fly you there. You leave immediately."

CHAPTER 19

German moaned knowingly. "You were in Norwich?"

"Yes," Knocker replied.

I knew what German was getting at and watched the scene play out before me. He said, "You were there when it happened?"

"Yes?"

"You were the cause?"

Knocker paused thoughtfully, then said, "Technically, not on my own."

"Do you realize what you have done?"

"I should, I was there."

"Over eight hundred years of history wiped out, just like that."

"I wouldn't call it wiped out," Knocker replied.

"Then, what would you bloody call it?!" German screeched.

"Fixable."

Trying to stifle a grin, I knew it wasn't funny, but I couldn't help it. Maybe one day I would go to hell for it. "Should we continue?"

"Yes, please," Christine Ryan said.

The helicopter flew me to Norwich, where I met up with Taras Granat. I suppose met is possibly too strong a word. It implies that we were there on mutual agreement. In fact, I was there because I needed to be, and he didn't want me there which caused us some issues later on. However, let's deal with the present.

Granat worked out of a small café that specialized in Russian cuisine. He was under sporadic surveillance by MI5, but for some reason, the surveillance had been pulled sometime within the past two weeks.

The café had a stone façade, its large windows trimmed with white. With no awning, the four tables outside the café were being splattered by an afternoon shower from the rock gray clouds overhead.

Having it under surveillance for the past hour, I was surprised to see nobody going in or out. Not even customers. I'm guessing it was one of the only cafés in the UK which made $1,000,000 per year without customers.

"Alpha, I'm going in."

"Roger," Holly replied. "Please try not to make a scene."

I chuckled. Couldn't help it. "Do we have eyes inside yet?"

"Nothing," Slick replied.

"All right, let's do this."

I left the doorway where I was hanging around and crossed the street in the rain, which was still coming up the Channel from the south. When I reached the opposite sidewalk, I went inside, pushing the door open which in turn rang the little bell hanging above it.

There were five people inside. None were customers. A woman stood behind the counter, sipping from a cup of something. Three others, undoubtedly bodyguards, were seated at a table, talking and looking through a shared newspaper. The last was Granat himself, seated alone and drinking coffee, reading his own paper.

He looked up at me as I walked toward him. I made it halfway to his table before a big Russian thug inserted himself in my line of travel, effectively stopping me. I say big, but he was about my size.

"What do you want?" he asked in heavily accented English. "We are closed."

"I didn't see no sign."

"Go away."

I glanced over at Granat, who was still looking at his own paper. "Got a moment, Taras?"

Showing no indication of having heard me, he continued perusing his paper. The big bodyguard standing in front of me spoke again. "Go away."

"Not until I see your boss."

"He doesn't want to see you."

I shrugged. "Let him tell me that."

The bodyguard pulled back the flap of his jacket, revealing a handgun. "Maybe you should change your mind."

"Is your dick that big?" I asked with a wry grin.

"Let him pass, Vladimir," Granat said.

"But, sir."

"Just do it. Once I have spoken with him, then you can kill him."

"Yes, sir." The big man stepped aside so I could pass.

Keeping an eye on the other bodyguards, I walked over to the table and sat down. Granat did not look up but seemed overly attentive to an article in the paper. He was consciously making me wait. My patience wore thin after a while, and I said, "Are you going to be much longer? I mean, if you are, I can speed things up a little. I don't have time to wait."

"You will wait as long as I see fit," he replied.

"I really don't want to."

Granat casually folded the paper, placed it neatly on the table, took a sip of his coffee, and then looked up at me. His actions were dragged out painfully, as if filmed in slow motion, and were starting to piss me off.

"What is it that you want?"

"Oleg Zhirkov."

I waited for his reaction, but his face remained passive. "I do not think I know that name."

"Okay, how about this? Bullshit."

"No, I do not think I know that name either."

"I already know that he and your father were friends. And if there's ever a time he needed a friend, it is now. So I'm telling you, he came to you and you've hidden him away until you can get him out of the country."

"You have a mighty imagination, my friend."

"Let me tell you something else. Zhirkov was part of a plan to take over the British government from the inside. That plan didn't work. How do I know? Because I killed the man they planted there."

That information elicited a reaction. If I had been

looking elsewhere, I would have missed the flicker in the old man's eyes, but it was there.

"We can do this the easy way or the hard way. Tell me the little bit of information I want to know now, or I can leave, come back, and go through this whole place with a fine-tooth comb and lock you up for good."

"You seem to think, my British friend, that you are leaving this place," Granat said.

I shook my head. "How about we start again? This time on much friendlier terms. Please, Mr. Granat, tell me what I need to know, and I will go away and leave you alone. I can't get much friendlier than that."

The woman from behind the counter placed a plate of food on the table in front of the Russian mob boss, laying cutlery beside him. He looked up and nodded. "Thank you."

Then he looked at Vladimir. "Get rid of him."

The big man moved.

So did I.

My left hand streaked across the table and my fingers grasped the knife. As I withdrew my arm, I brought it around in an arc just as Vladimir leaned over to drag me from my seat. The knife plunged deep into his left eye socket. Using my right hand, the heel of my palm hit the handle of the knife, driving it deeper. My left hand went inside his jacket after his handgun as the big man stumbled then fell backward.

The gun came free, and I took a punt that there was a round in the breech. I aimed and squeezed the trigger at another guard who was responding. The weapon bucked in my hand, so I fired again.

The bodyguard fell, taking a table with him. This left the third guy. "No, mate, just let it go."

He snarled and tried anyway. So, I was compelled to shoot him. This time, only in the shoulder. It caused him to drop his weapon and fall backward over his chair. In the process of all this, I came to my feet and walked over to the fallen man. I kicked his weapon away and said, "Just stay there."

Now I turned my attention back to Granat. "Right, let's talk."

He glanced around the room before bringing his tired gaze back to me. "What do you want to know?"

"Where is Zhirkov?"

"He is at the Norwich Cathedral."

"The cathedral?"

"It is a place of sanctuary for many. The dean is from the motherland."

"So Zhirkov is hiding there?"

"Yes. When the cathedral was originally constructed, a subterranean area was built as well. That is where he will be."

As I began to turn away, Granat said, "Good luck. You will need it."

"Luck has nothing to do with it."

Heading back to the SUV, I used my phone to Google the cathedral, wanting to see what I was walking into. Slick was my next contact to get schematics of the basement area if he could access them. Then I drove the short distance to the cathedral and parked the SUV. I checked the loads in my Glock and climbed out, tucking the weapon in the back of my pants. Pushing through the large doors, I went inside.

I'd had occasion to enter many a nice church in my time, but this was something else. When I stepped into the nave, I was awestruck by its height and grandeur. The ceiling was vaulted and supported by tall columns.

My eyes were drawn to the large, stained-glass windows—in summertime, the sun would fill the place with colored light. The walls held a myriad of medieval artworks, and there were other treasures scattered throughout. Everything had to be worth a fortune.

A pew was receiving loving ministrations from a woman with a soft cloth and wood polish, and I walked over to her. "I'm looking for the dean."

Glancing at me warily, she murmured, "He is in the catacombs."

The chapel's undercroft, originally used as a charnel house to store the bones of the faithful awaiting the resurrection, was public knowledge. However, the catacombs beneath were not as well publicized. Less well known was the fact that they had been converted to a subterranean base of operations for the Russians. It was also where Zhirkov and those of his people had taken sanctuary until they could get out of the UK.

I stared at her. "Show me."

The woman led me through the cathedral to a large door that opened at the head of a spiral staircase. "Down there."

Nodding my thanks, I said, "You'd better leave. Take the rest of the day off."

She gave me a strange look. I shrugged and began making my way downstairs.

The staircase led me into a large underground room. The room appeared to be normal catacombs with other tunnels branching off it. The whole thing was constructed of ancient stone and old brick, and the air smelled damp.

There was movement off to my right, and a man appeared from one of the tunnels in that direction. He paused and stared at me. "Who are you?"

"Are you the dean?" I asked him.

"Yes."

"Great, I was told you were down here."

"What do you want?"

"I was hoping to talk to you about a funeral service," I replied.

"I'm not the one—a funeral service?"

"Yes."

"Whose?"

I brought the Glock up from behind my back and said, "Yours if you don't give me what I want."

His hands went up and he took a defensive posture. "What are you doing?"

The weapon was unwavering. "I'm looking for Oleg Zhirkov."

His eyes revealed it immediately, despite the lie flowing seamlessly from his lips. "I have never heard of him."

"Now are you sure you want to go down this path, mate?" I asked him.

"My name is—"

"I don't need to know your name," I told him. "I'm sure those who erect your headstone will know it."

He paled. "I already—"

I stepped forward and hit him between the eyes with the butt of my Glock. Not hard enough to knock him out, but enough to split the skin there. He dropped to a knee, blood streaming from the wound.

Stepping in close, I grabbed a handful of hair and pulled his head back. "Now, mate, let's try again."

That was when the problems started. The dean was a little overweight, and apparently, being a Russian operative didn't exempt him from having a heart condition. Even through the flow of the blood, I could see there was a problem. Then he clutched at his chest, mouth agape, fear in his eyes.

"Are you having a heart attack on me?" I asked him.

Without a word, the dean grew heavy in my grasp and slumped over.

"Yeah, of course you fucking are." I looked up. "Shit—sorry, Father."

And he died. There was nothing I could do about it.

Leaving his body lying on the cold, damp flagstone floor, I stepped away, looking around. I probably would have shot him anyway, but the fear on his face as he was having his heart attack actually rather disturbed me. I looked to the tunnel from which he'd emerged and walked toward it. The passageway was illuminated by evenly spaced lights along the ceiling.

The first heavy wooden door I came to was on my right and I stopped to listen before opening it. The room beyond was filled with crates. Curious, I stepped inside and closed the door. The first crate I opened revealed automatic weapons. AK-12s. The second was more of the same. The third held magazines of ammunition. I looked into another and found fragmentation grenades. Who would have thought that something as serene and grand as the Norwich Cathedral would be hiding such a deathly secret in its deep, dark depths.

Not one to look a gift horse in the mouth, I filled my pockets with a few grenades and picked up an AK. Moving to another crate, I selected several magazines, cramming them into my pants before leaving the room.

I hadn't gone very far before an armed man appeared. He shouted in surprise and brought his weapon around. It was a race to see who could fire first. Both weapons leveled, and it was what one might refer to as fastest finger.

And it wasn't me. But fortunately, the shooter was too quick on the trigger and his burst missed, flying wide. Mine took his legs out from under him because I'd fired too fast as well.

Hot on the heels of the echoing gunfire, the man let out a howl of pain as he fell to the hard floor. His weapon tumbled from his hands with a loud rattle. I moved forward, aiming the AK in my hand at his head. Then I shot him.

Without hesitation, I moved on. Ahead of me, the tunnel curved to the left and I followed it, almost walking into a wall of gunfire.

Bullets hammered into the curved stone surface beside me, making me pivot back into cover. "Shit, that was close."

Another fusillade came my way, and then I heard shouts from at least three more shooters. I glanced around the corner of the passage and saw men leapfrogging each other. Bullets kept coming like a persistent curtain of rain.

I ducked back, drew a breath, and then leaned back around and opened fire. My own hailstorm of bullets cut through the air and found flesh. A cry of pain brought forth an even more savage storm, forcing me back.

Muttering a curse, I was about to send forth more fire when I heard a familiar rattle at my feet. Without needing to look, I instantly knew what it was and began to run, throwing myself to the floor further along the tunnel just as the grenade exploded.

With ringing ears, I had to admit that the explosion had rocked me a little as the heat from the blast washed over me. I willed myself to move and crawled along the floor, making it back to the doorway where the weapons and ammunition were stored. I ducked inside and pressed my back against the wall near the opening.

Reaching for my own fragmentation grenades, I knew I needed to somehow hold them back to enable my escape. I pulled the pin and threw it along the hallway. Then I ducked back and waited.

The explosion rocked the catacombs, and I heard more cries of pain. Then I ran once more to the steps which took me up into the cathedral proper.

My thoughts that I would somehow be safe there were erroneous. There was more than one passage up from the catacombs. A team had been sent forth, and they were moving in to flank me. I saw them coming and threw myself down behind a pew.

The flankers opened fire, and bullets ripped through the cathedral, splintering wood and hammering the walls. The priceless artwork up behind me disintegrated. Hundreds of thousands of dollars gone just like that.

Returning their fire, I saw one of them fall, then switched my aim, and the next guy went down. By now, however, the remnants of the group I had engaged in the tunnel downstairs were reaching the top of the stairs, and I was in even more trouble.

From my position behind the bullet-scarred pew, I bounded backward over it and launched myself to the right, running for one of the pillars that held the ceiling up. Bullets peppered the sandstone, leaving deep scars. I fired once more, but the AK magazine ran dry.

Pulling back, the empty magazine dropped at my feet, and I reloaded, catching a glimpse of a shooter trying to flank my position. I swung the AK around and fired in his direction.

The first burst missed, taking out a vase of flowers and a bust. I muttered a curse and fired again. This time, my accuracy improved. I hit him, and he fell back. He reflexively squeezed the trigger, and a long burst blasted from the weapon as he went. Bullets peppered the ornate ceiling, leaving terrible scars. But worse than that was the damage done to the stained-glass windows, a shower of colored glass falling to the floor below.

Frustration emanated from my throat in a sonorous growl. I was now pinned down and under heavy fire. There was nothing else for it. I reached into my pocket.

"Mr. Jensen, please don't tell us that you actually threw a grenade inside the Norwich Cathedral," German said.

"No, sir, I didn't throw one at all."

"That is a relief."

The pins slipped from the two grenades with ease. I threw one in each direction. You can guess what happened next.

By the time the smoke and dust began to clear, a good portion of the ceiling had come down, along with some other things. It didn't do the pipe organ much good either. It was at about that moment that I knew I was definitely going to hell. But not just yet.

I stepped from behind the pillar and scanned for targets. Any targets. I found one crawling through the debris, missing a good part of his leg. I shot him in the back of the head and his brains painted the floor. I saw another, but he was dead, like many of the others.

One appeared from behind a pillar and commenced firing in my direction. I shot back movie style. From the hip—just sprayed him with what was left in the magazine. He cried out and fell face down.

Then I saw the man of the hour walking from the carnage and destruction. Oleg Zhirkov was battered, limping, and bloody. I think that maybe they were trying to get him out the other way rather than trap me.

He caught sight of me coming toward him through the rubble. In his hand was a gun. He raised it and fired, his hand trembling. The shot went wide. He fired again. The result was the same.

"It's done, Oleg. Time to give it over."

"Give what over?" he snarled.

My Glock came up, and I said, "Your life."

Then I shot him.

———

Not my finest moment I'll admit, but the threat was neutralized. I'd disappeared by the time the scene was sealed off. MI6 flew me back to London, and I was met there by a less-than-happy Christine Ryan and an even more savage ex-wife.

"What the fuck was that?" Miriam hissed at me. "You just blew the shit out of a national monument."

"Yeah, sorry about that."

"Sorry? Is that all you have to say for yourself?"

I shrugged.

"I must say, Mr. Jensen, you really have outdone all previous attempts to fuck up," Christine Ryan said, joining the party.

"I do try."

"Bloody hell," Miriam snarled. "I will see that you are locked away for this. And I will personally turn the bloody key."

"I don't think they use keys these days, Miriam," I pointed out.

"Shut up!"

"Ma'am."

"Do you realize how much time and money it will take to rebuild the portion of the cathedral you demolished? Do you?"

I remained silent.

"Christ, I knew you were a screw-up from the get-go, but this...this..."

"I believe you are looking for—"

"Shut up! I know what I'm looking for."

It was Holly who saved the day. She opened the door and interrupted my castigation ceremony, saying, "Kane is missing. Time to get back to work."

CHAPTER 20

"THIS IS TED AND CRAMER," HOLLY SAID, GESTURING TO two men who followed her into the room. "They'll be helping you."

Ted was new to me, but Cramer, I knew. "Cramer."

"Knocker. They tell me your boy is missing."

"He has a tendency of doing shit like that."

"Don't I know it?"

"These men worked with John in Cuba," Holly explained.

"What do we know?" I asked.

"Kane was taken by Russian forces while on his way to Helsinki, where he was trying to locate Morozov. At this point in time, we have no idea where they took him, but we're reasonably sure he is in the capital."

"What is the situation like in the city?" I asked Holly.

"The Russians have captured a good portion of it while NATO is attempting to gain control of the skies. Neither British nor US forces are fully engaged yet, but they're getting there. SAS and SBS are deployed and are already raiding certain targets in the area. The SBS attacked a cross-bay ferry operation the Russians were utilizing and sank it at the dock. They also planted charges on ammunition stocks and demolished them as well."

Slick appeared. "Ma'am, we've got a location of the assets on the ground."

I looked at Holly. "What assets?"

"Technically, they're not really assets but will suffice as they're all we have. Manuela Garza works with GROM. I brought her in to help John in Cuba. The other is a reporter. Hatti Gibson works with NBC. There was also a camera guy with her, but he was killed."

"So, we're going to get them out and find Reaper too?"

"That's the plan."

"Then let's do it."

———

We were inserted by an underwater delivery vehicle piloted by a couple of SBS guys. Our jumping-off point was Estonia. Reaching Helsinki, we managed to get ashore, where Hatti and Manuela were waiting for us in the shadows.

A lot had happened in the past twenty-four hours. NATO planes were taking back the airspace over Finland and their troops were pressing hard on the city to link up. The Russians couldn't hold.

"I want to stay," Manuela insisted.

I shook my head. "The boss insisted on getting you back to London to be debriefed."

"Damn it—"

"I don't have time to argue," I told her. "Get your ass on the UDV and go."

Just minutes later, the pair had gone.

"Alpha, Bravo is feet dry and moving to the next waypoint. Anything to report yet?"

"Roger, Bravo. We might have something, just need to confirm it. Proceed on task."

"Copy."

Cramer, Ted, and I moved out through the darkness. In the distance, I could hear the staccato sound of gunfire, occasionally punctuated by a deep blast. We moved closer to the battle zone even though we were already behind enemy lines.

Slick said, "Bravo, we've found him. Sending coordinates now."

"Roger that. Well done."

The coordinates came through and the dot pinged on a police station about a klick from where we stood. Ted led the way, traversing streets that had already seen battle. The buildings were damaged, and the streets were littered with debris and the occasional corpse.

Most of the civilians had fled the city. They had flooded out when the Russian forces had invaded and were now displaced, taking refuge in the surrounding countryside. It had become a ruthless battle for control.

A little before two in the morning, we found the police station. As we watched, we picked out the guards. There were four on the perimeter that we could see, and there were supposedly another five or six on the inside.

I said into my comms, "Alpha, copy?"

"Copy, Bravo."

"Can we confirm that Morozov is on site?"

"Negative, Bravo. We think that Morozov and the mercenary Grigori Igoshin have left the city for Moscow. We also believe that those remaining on site are Igoshin's own people."

"Roger that." I turned to Cramer. "Let's do this."

Breaching the perimeter, using our suppressed G36Ks, we took out the guards. I managed to bag one while Ted and Cramer cleaned up the other three. We then pressed on toward the station and entered right through the front door.

With our surprise complete, we had the building secured within five minutes.

———

When I busted into Kane's cell, I had the last guard tucked under my arm. I took one look at Reaper and grinned as I shot the guard in the head.

"Hello, Reaper, old mate. How the fuck are you?"

Cramer and Ted pushed in beside me. Cramer said, "Ted, check him out before we move him."

Kane stared at me, his gaze seeming to swim as he tried to focus. "Where the fuck have you been?"

"Saving the world, old cock. Hard fucking job to do on your own."

"Manuela," he said. "She—"

"She's in London, mate. We got her and the reporter out. You're it."

Reaper tried to stand, but Ted held him in position. "Ease up, mate, I'm not finished."

Cramer's head dipped as he listened to an incoming transmission. Once it was done, he lifted his head. "All right, gentlemen, it's time to go. Ted, wrap it up."

Kane got to his feet with the help of Ted. Then I took over from there. "I've got you, Reaper. Let's get the fuck out of here."

"What about Igoshin and Morozov?" he asked.

"Rats deserting a sinking ship, mate," I replied. "Everything is closing in on them, so they bailed."

"This doesn't end while they are all still alive," he said.

"We'll get them. You just need to be squared away first."

We humped to the extraction point and waited for a helicopter to come in. Once it touched down, we climbed aboard and got the hell out of dodge.

———

Kane spent the next two days in a hospital at Ramstein while I rode shotgun. It was discussed whether or not to send him back to London, but getting his system clean was the primary concern.

The ward person brought him in a meal. It remained uneaten in front of him for about ten minutes. I nodded at it. "You going to eat that?"

Reaper shook his head. "Nope."

Pulling the plate toward me, I began hooking in. It was touted to be beef and vegetables. I took two mouthfuls and said, "Tastes like camel shit."

"Then don't eat it."

I took another forkful. "I'm hungry."

He shook his head at me. I'm sure he was about to say something when his cell rang. Kane looked at it and then at me. I said, "Are you going to answer it, or what?"

He nodded slowly before picking it up and hitting the answer button. "Kane."

I watched his face as he listened to the person on the other end. When it was over, he stared at me for a few moments, then said, "He wants to meet."

"Who?"

"Shatov."

"Our Shatov?"

"Yes. He says it's urgent."

"What could be so urgent?"

"Something called Hephaestus."

"Shit."

"Yes, shit."

"That should bring us to another close for today," German *said to us as Knocker finished. "We'll pick it up again tomorrow. I think it will only need one more day."*

"And we should find out more of this Hephaestus," Holland *said.*

"There is still one more thing," Christine Ryan *said. "The mystery that is Hecate."*

"Tomorrow," I replied. *"It'll all become clearer then."*

"Fine. All right, until then."

We left the room and made our way outside to the steps, where we stood discussing the events of the day. Moments later, Newman joined us. "I won't come in first thing tomorrow. I'll hang back and come when it is time."

"Are we sure he's going to do it?" Holly *asked.*

"He'll do it," I replied. "Ken?"

Newman nodded. "Yes, he'll do it."

"Then it'll be over."

We were about to walk away when a black sedan pulled up at the curb in front of us. The window came down, revealing the face of Miriam Craig. She said, "I was hoping you'd be finished."

Knocker stared at her. "Why, so you can castrate me and gnaw on my bollocks?"

"I was thinking dinner at Number Ten."

He looked at us and said, "I'll see you all later."

"You're actually going?" I asked.

"It is a free feed, after all."

I watched as he climbed in on the other side, and then the vehicle drove away. That left me, Newman, and Holly. It was Newman who said, "Beer?"

"Yes, why not?"

As we started walking away from the building, Holly asked, "How do you figure tomorrow is going to go?"

"Interesting," I replied. "It's going to be very interesting."

WATCH FOR WAR OF THE IMMORTALS (THE GODS OF WAR 6)

A line has been drawn, and millions will die if they fail...

Kane and Jensen reunite in their most perilous mission yet, one that will determine the fate of millions. A deadly nuclear weapon, codenamed Hephaestus, has fallen into dangerous hands, and the newly elected Russian president is ready to deploy it. With a small country on the brink of annihilation, the stakes couldn't be higher.

But the threat doesn't end there. Hecate, a cunning Russian mole, is lurking in the shadows, sabotaging their every move as they race across Europe to stop the impending catastrophe.

Time is running out. As the clock ticks down, Kane and Jensen must confront both an enemy with unimaginable power and the ultimate betrayal in a twist that will leave you breathless.

Can Kane and Jensen save millions before it's too late? Packed with relentless action, international intrigue, and a jaw-dropping conclusion, this high-octane thriller will keep you turning pages until the very end.

AVAILABLE DECEMBER 2024

ABOUT THE AUTHOR

A relative newcomer to the world of writing, Brent Towns self-published his first book in 2015. Last Stand in Sanctuary took him two years to write. His first hardcover book, a Black Horse Western, was published the following year.

Since then, he has written twenty-six western stories, including some in collaboration with British western author, Ben Bridges; several action adventure novels, such as his bestselling Team Reaper series; the novelization to the 2019 movie, Bill Tilghman and the Outlaws; as well as scripted a handful of Commando Comics. Not bad for an Australian author, he thinks.

Often up until the small hours of the night, bashing away at his tortured keyboard in Queensland, Australia, Brent loves to lose himself in the world of fiction. If you're interested in sharing your thoughts in more detail, scan the QR code below! Your feedback is invaluable to him—and often helps shape his future writing endeavors.